The Body

She lay between two trees, not ten feet from the pond, from myself. Her hair was blond; she appeared to be about seventeen or eighteen. She lay on her back, her right leg twisted beneath her body at an unnatural angle. Her left hand touched the closest tree, held up by the trunk rather than her own musculature. The expression on her face was one of shock; her open blue eyes stared at the black sky without blinking. Of course, it would have been frightening to see her blink when it looked as if she had been stabbed a dozen times in the chest and abdomen. Her yellow sweater was so red it could have been a Christmas gift from a psychotic Santa. Even her blue jeans were drenched in blood. There was no need to check on her breathing, her heartbeat. No one would be hanging a stocking at the fireplace for her this holiday season.

In the grass, close to where I sat, was a knife.

A bloody blade. It was *so* close.

While I slept, it could have fallen from my hand.

"Oh God," I whispered.

Books by Christopher Pike

Christopher PIKE

The Lost Mind

AN ARCHWAY PAPERBACK
Published by POCKET BOOKS
New York   London   Toronto   Sydney   Tokyo   Singapore

This book is a work of fiction. Names, characters, places and incidents are products of the author's imagination or are used fictitiously. Any resemblance to actual events or locales or persons, living or dead, is entirely coincidental.

AN ARCHWAY PAPERBACK *Original*

An Archway Paperback published by
POCKET BOOKS, a division of Simon & Schuster Inc.
1230 Avenue of the Americas, New York, NY 10020

Copyright © 1995 by Christopher Pike

ISBN: 0-671-87269-9

First Archway Paperback printing August 1995

10 9 8 7 6 5 4 3 2 1

AN ARCHWAY PAPERBACK and colophon are registered trademarks of Simon & Schuster Inc.

Stepback art by Mark Garro

Printed in the U.S.A.

For Gina Gehrke

The Lost Mind

CHAPTER 1

THE FIRST THING I FELT WHEN I AWOKE WAS THE cold. It was as if my body were resting on a hard slab of ice. I could have been a corpse, locked in freezing storage, awaiting a clinical autopsy or burial. There was something besides the chill of the awakening that was peculiar. I felt as if I had been unconscious for a long time. Dead even— someone or some*thing* that was never supposed to return to the living world.

My eyes popped open, and I saw I was lying on the ground beside a pond. It was dark; moonlight shimmered on the surface of the water like rays beamed to earth from an alien world. The water was remarkably clear. The smooth stones on the floor of the pond, the tendrils of green algae—

they were distinctly visible. Yet dark shadows moved in the fresh fluid like floating spirits escaping from graves. Stabbed through with moonlight, the shadows took on a reddish hue.

I realized I was looking at blood.

I sat up quickly.

"Where am I?" I said out loud.

The sound of my own voice startled me.

I didn't recognize it.

But the sticky red fluid was easy to recognize. Not only did it cloud the pond, it was all over my arms, my chest, my clothes. I was soaked in blood. Yet, as I examined myself, I could find only two small cuts on the back of my right hand. True, one was deep, and still bleeding, but neither had spilled a tenth of the blood that I could see. Taking in the fact that I was sitting alone in a small clearing deep in the woods at night, I scanned the trees and bushes for another source of the blood.

My gaze didn't have to travel far.

She lay between two trees, not ten feet from the pond, from myself. Her hair was blond; she appeared to be about seventeen or eighteen. She lay on her back, her right leg twisted beneath her body at an unnatural angle. Her left hand touched the closest tree, held up by the trunk rather than her own musculature. The expression on her face was one of shock; her open blue eyes stared at the black sky without blinking. Of course, it would have been frightening to see her blink when it looked as if she had been stabbed a dozen times in the chest and abdomen. Her yellow sweater was so red it could have been a Christmas gift from a psychotic Santa. Even her blue jeans were drenched in blood. There was no need to check on her breathing, her heartbeat. No one would be hanging a stocking at the fireplace for her this holiday season.

In the grass, close to where I sat, was a knife. A bloody blade. It was *so* close.

While I slept, it could have fallen from my hand.

"Oh God," I whispered.

I didn't recognize the young woman. I didn't recognize my surroundings. Frantically, I tried to think of where I'd been last, who I'd been with. But nothing came to me. Nothing at all. Not even what day it was. What state I was in. What year it was.

It was then I realized that I didn't know who I was.

"But I must know," I told myself.

As I said the words, I realized I didn't know who I said them to.

I was so cold that I had to be in shock. That was why I couldn't remember anything. I had to get to my feet. Get my circulation going. Get out of this place. A young woman had been murdered. The killer might still be in the area. He might return, carve me up. It was a small miracle he hadn't killed me while he was killing the blond girl.

After climbing unsteadily to my feet, I felt myself over again. Basically, I was uninjured. Just messy. With the girl's blood. But how had I gotten her blood all over me?

I shuddered to think of the possibilities. But at the same time there seemed no possibilities. Certainly I hadn't killed her. I may not have been able to remember who I was, but I knew I was no murderer. I had never hurt a soul in my life.

I turned to flee.

Then I stopped.

I couldn't leave her alone like this, at least not without checking on her.

Moving silently, in case I'd mysteriously raise her from her dead sleep, I stepped to the girl's side and looked down. Her pale blue eyes stared up at me. She was a pretty girl, or had been, with high cheekbones, a large sensuous mouth, a button nose. But her expression, seen from close up, was not so much one of shock but of horror. She had not died easily. Worse, perhaps, she had died not knowing why she was being killed.

I knelt and took her hand. It was cold, naturally. Yet the flesh and blood that covered her arms was slightly warmer than the ground. I was no coroner but I'd guess she hadn't been dead that long. Two hours maybe. Had I been unconscious the same length of time? Had she been killed before I lost consciousness? What had knocked me out anyway?

Disturbing questions.

"I'm sorry," I whispered suddenly, not intending to speak. I mean, I was sorry she was dead, that I had nothing to cover her with. I wasn't apologizing for killing her. I hadn't killed her. It was inconceivable.

My eyes strayed back to the knife.

Maybe it had only slipped from my hand when I woke up.

That meant—nothing! Whoever killed the girl placed the knife in my hand after I'd lost consciousness. He wanted to make it look as if I'd killed her. There was no other explanation.

Still, I didn't want to leave the area without the knife.

If I ran into the murderer, I might need it.

And it probably had *my* fingerprints all over it.

For a moment I was torn between staying and leaving. Now that I had stared into the girl's eyes, it was hard to leave her side. To abandon her to the ants and spiders and little animals that would surely begin to crawl in her mouth, over her face, nibbling at her eyeballs. It was too horrible to contemplate! Yet the more I looked at the knife, the more I was seized by a desire to grab the weapon and leave. The girl was dead—God save her soul—but there was nothing I could do for her. But the knife was a problem. Something could be done about that. Once clear of the area, I could throw it away.

"Or bury it," I whispered before I realized what I was saying.

The knife was a weapon of murder. If I hid it, I could prevent the police from finding the murderer, prosecuting him successfully. I shouldn't take it, I knew. I should disturb the crime scene as little as possible. Of course, once I talked to the police, I would have a hard time explaining where it had been when I woke up, why I had handled it. Maybe I could leave out that little detail. I could say the knife was just lying on the ground beside the girl. Before I left, I could wipe it off and drop it beside her head. No harm done.

I stepped over and picked up the knife.

It would have been scary even without blood all over it. The blade was stainless steel, six inches of razor-sharp pain. Turning it over in my hand, I watched the cool metal glimmer in the harsh moonlight. The edge was jagged, used for cutting and hacking. It was a hunting knife and it had been used to go hunting.

Why had this girl died?

Why had someone wanted her dead?

Without thinking, I stashed the knife in my back pocket.

I just needed time. To sort this out.

To remember who I was.

The police could have the knife later.

Once more I stepped to the girl's side. Her vacant eyes continued to stare up at the stars, the endless blackness. A tear touched my cold cheek. I had never seen her before, I was quite sure. She was not my friend. But I could tell, seeing beyond her twisted features, that she had been a kind person. Someone who had loved life, and been loved. At that moment I wept for her and those who may have loved her. God, how would her parents feel when they learned she was dead?

Gently, I leaned over and closed her eyes.

"We'll come back for you soon," I promised.

I turned and walked into the forest.

I tried not to look back. Tried.

The woods were lush. The tall pines and thick bushes pushed in on me like a bustling crowd. The hanging branches clawed at my hair, the skin on my arms. I had no idea where I was going, and after going there for half an hour, I realized I was completely lost. Fortunately the walking had warmed me up some. Stopping to study the stars, to try to get my bearings, I felt in the right pocket of my jeans. There was a bulge there. Exploring farther I found a set of keys. Three keys on a plain chain.

It was surely chance, but right then I heard a car go by, caught the faint glimmer of headlights off to my left. My heart leapt in my chest and I hurried in that direction.

Ten minutes later I came to a two-lane road. On a hill. Up appeared to lead deeper into the forest. In the other direction there was a faint glow in the sky. A city, still partially awake this late at night. Of course I had no watch, no wallet. I didn't know what time it was, and I didn't know the name of this city. Yet I began to walk down the road, toward it. The knife still in my pocket. The girl's blood still coating my hands, arms, and clothes.

I felt exposed on the road. Guilty.

Twenty minutes later I came to a parked car. A blue Toyota Celica, parked with its nose heading up a hill. I removed the keys from my pocket. I remembered one was a key for a Toyota. When I slipped the key in the door lock it opened. This must be my car, I thought.

But I didn't recognize it. Not even vaguely.

What kind of amnesia was this? As I opened the car door, I knew I would have no trouble driving. I had not forgotten the basics of life. I knew the earth was the third planet from the sun.

I knew about MTV. Which bands were popular. What french fries tasted like, and even how it felt to make love. I was not a virgin visitor to this planet. Yet, as I studied the interior of the car, I saw nothing that stimulated even a faint remembrance of my past life. It was as if my soul had entered my body the moment I awoke beside that pool of water.

I started to get in the car. Then stopped. Thinking.

If I just got in and drove away, I'd get blood all over the seats. They were covered with fabric, not leather. The stains wouldn't come out, not easily. And the blood did not belong to me. I had not spilled it, but if I drenched the car, it would look like I had. Later, I would have trouble explaining that as well. I would have to start by telling the police I didn't know who I was, assuming of course that my memory didn't come back. Likely story, they'd say. I'd have trouble finding a lawyer to represent me.

There was no extra clothing lying over the front- or backseat—only a coat. I decided to check the trunk. There was a pair of clean gray sweats that looked like they'd fit. Why not? They were in *my* trunk.

I couldn't just put them on, however. The blood would get all over them. While wandering around in the woods, I had passed several pools of water. None as large as the pond where I had waked up, but a few with sufficient water to wash and clean up. After carefully picking up the sweats with the tips of my fingers, I closed the trunk and walked back into the woods.

I found a tiny pond fifty feet from the road. The water was freezing cold like the night air. I stripped down, removing everything, including my underwear. Splashing myself all over, I began to shiver furiously. The blood washed easily from my skin, but my hair was a problem. Kneeling down and leaning over, I had to duck my head in the icy pool to get it clean. The moon was almost directly overhead by then and I got a jolt when I rose up from the pond. A pale ghost jumped up at me. No, my reflection did, but it looked like a ghost. A naked soul rising from an unclean coffin. The fright caused my heart to pound wildly but even that didn't stop me from shivering.

Not waiting to dry off, I pulled on the gray sweats and slipped my shoes back on, minus socks. My bloody clothes I carried back to the car. I remembered there had been a blanket in the trunk. I could wrap them in that, I thought, and get rid of them later. The knife I also wrapped in the clothes. God knew what I was going to do with it.

A few minutes later I sat in the car with the

engine running, the heater on full, the lights out. The Celica was relatively new; the heater worked well. I was soon dry, warm. It was only then I turned on the dome light and looked at myself in the vanity mirror.

My face, my own face, did not look familiar.

My hair was brown, long, fine as a child's. My eyes were also brown, innocent and clear, except for the bloodshot that stained the corners. There was an easiness to my features, no deep lines of trauma. My life had obviously not been hard. I appeared to be intelligent. Like the dead girl's, my lips were full. But I didn't know about my teeth, and did not feel like flashing a smile to check on them. I was attractive, but not beautiful by any stretch of the imagination. There was no blood on me. Inside or out.

"I couldn't have killed her," I muttered.

There was nothing but the coat on the seats, front or back. I felt under the driver's seat. When my fingers brushed a purse, I froze. It was likely that the purse belonged to me, and that it had my identification inside. It was a big step to look at a picture with my name beside it. I didn't know if I wanted to take such a step. Despite all the horror I was going through, I was not freaked out. Indeed, I had handled things wisely so far, in my opinion. And I thought part of the reason was because there was so little of me inside for the horror to reverberate with. There was safety in being a no one.

Still, I had to know.

I slipped the purse out and opened it.

Inside were a few dollars, thirty maybe. Two credit cards. I didn't look too closely at the name on them. The driver's license caught my attention. It had my picture on it. A few other details: Height 5' 4"; Weight 110.

Name.

Jennifer Hobbs. Me.

I had never heard of the person.

I sat staring at the picture on the license for a long time.

"Jennifer," I whispered. "Jenny."

Nothing rang familiar in my ears. In my heart.

If the information on the license was current, I lived at 1666 Red Coach Lane, Carlsrue, Oregon. I knew about the State of Oregon but had never heard of Carlsrue. It didn't sound like a city I'd live in. But then, too, was a Celica a car I'd buy? I didn't know. When I stopped to think about it, I had no personal tastes. Except as far as the basics were concerned. I liked food, music, sex, being warm. But what kind of food did I like? What kind of music? What kind of guys?

It was as if all the things that made me an individual were gone.

"But I am human," I told myself. "Jennifer is human."

And a sane human being would not kill another human being.

Not unless it was absolutely necessary.

Setting the purse, the license, aside, I put the car in gear.

Up or down? I wondered for an instant. North or south?

There was really only one choice.

I headed for the city.

Maybe it was Carlsrue.

CHAPTER 2

THERE WAS A SIGN AS I ROLLED INTO TOWN, TEN MILES later. "Carlsrue: Population 31,876. Welcome." This was home, but it didn't feel like it. As I coasted through the dark streets, I failed to recognize a single building. Where was Red Coach Lane? Maybe I'd already passed it. There was a phone booth up ahead, an open Shell station. I pulled over and stopped. There was a checkbook in my purse, with a phone number on it. Jenny Hobbs's number. I found some change in the glove compartment and climbed out into the brisk air to call home. I prayed the person who answered knew me. And I also prayed that he or she didn't know me.

I got an answering machine.

"Hi, this is Jenny. Please leave your name and number and a detailed physical description, and I'll call you back. Ciao!"

I hung up and talked to myself.

"Hi, this is Jenny. Please leave your name and number and a detailed physical description, and I'll call you back. Ciao."

I sounded like her. Only not as happy.

The Jenny who had recorded the message had never woken up soaked with blood.

Once more I picked up the phone and dialed Information, asking for the Hobbses' residence on Red Coach Lane. Two numbers were listed. I took the one I didn't know, which I assumed was my parents' number. My hand shook as I dialed the number. What was I going to say? Hello, Mom. Who are you?

A tired-sounding woman answered the phone. "Hello?"

I hesitated. "Hi. It's me."

"Jenny? Where have you been? I've been waiting up for you."

"I've just been out, you know, goofing off."

"Do you know what time it is?"

"No. I mean, yeah. I'm sorry."

"Are you with Crystal?"

I hoped I hadn't been with Crystal. "No."

"Her mother called. She was looking for her."

"I'm sure she's fine." I paused. "Don't worry, go to bed. I'll be home in a little bit."

The woman, my mother, paused. "Are you sure you're all right?"

"Yeah. I'm fine, really. Go to sleep."

Another pause. "I'll see you in the morning, Jenny."

"Good night," I said gently.

I hung up the phone. I was shaking like a leaf.

I didn't want to go home immediately because I wanted to make sure I gave my mother—how strange that sounded—time to fall asleep. Also I needed to get a map of the area to find out where Red Coach Lane was. Pocketing my remaining change, I walked over to the window of the gas station. The guy on duty was reading a *Penthouse* magazine. Without looking up, he slid me a local map. Carlsrue was not very big. It took me only two minutes to figure out how to get home. With the guy's permission, I took the map with me. It also wasn't too hard to figure out where my car had been parked, and approximately where the girl's body lay. I had wandered around lost for half an hour in the woods but I suspected I had walked in circles. From the map I could tell I had never been more than a mile and a half from the road, probably less.

Getting back in my car, I decided to drive

around town for a while, get to know the place again. But my stomach was grumbling. I was hungry and thirsty. Not long after leaving the gas station, I spotted a Denny's. Open twenty-four hours. I parked and went inside, not forgetting that I had bloody clothes and a knife in my trunk.

The place was largely empty. There was a clock near the cash register.

Two-fifteen in the morning.

No wonder my mother had been worried.

A waitress at the far end of the Denny's waved to me. She must know me. I waved back. After refilling a gentleman's coffee cup, she bustled over.

"What are you doing here now, Jen?" she asked. Her name tag said Elaine. She was short, chubby. Her squat dark legs looked as if she used them to store emergency food rations. Her face, also heavy, was pleasant enough. The way she looked at me indicated she liked me.

And Elaine would have nothing to do with a murderer.

I shrugged. "Just out and about. Couldn't sleep."

She looked past me, to the door. "Is Crystal with you?"

"No."

Elaine chuckled. "I hardly see you two guys apart. Where do you want to sit?"

17

I nodded to a corner booth. "Over there would be fine."

Elaine led me to the table. She didn't offer me a menu. "The usual?" she asked.

I sat down. "Sure." It would be interesting to see what that was.

While waiting for my order, I picked up a piece of the local paper. The big news was a councilman's tax fraud. Carlsrue was not a happening place. The date was November 22.

The deep cut on my right hand continued to bleed slightly. I applied pressure to it with a paper napkin and then stuffed the bloody paper in my pocket. Elaine returned ten minutes later.

"Apple pie à la mode," she said as she placed the plate in front of me. "Unheated. Decaf coffee. Will there be anything else, miss?"

I forced a smile. "No, thank you." I paused, and she turned away. "Elaine?"

She glanced over her shoulder. "Yeah?"

"Was Crystal in here earlier?"

"No. I didn't see her. Why?"

"Just wondering."

Elaine had a customer waiting. "Enjoy the calories."

"I will," I said.

In fact, I did enjoy the pie. Clearly it was a while since I'd eaten. Twice Elaine refilled my cup, and it was a pleasure to have the hot liquid sink into my body. While I ate, several more customers came in, and Elaine was suddenly very busy. I paid and left without really speaking to her.

Before going home, I cruised behind a closed supermarket. A metal Dumpster stood beside the receiving dock. After removing a flashlight from my glove compartment, I climbed up the side of the huge garbage can to search for a bag of some type. I could see about a dozen of them mixed in with the flattened boxes and discarded food, the big green kind. Looking around to make sure no one was watching, I dropped down into the garbage. The odor was manageable, but I hoped my mother was not waiting up to smell me when I came through the front door.

I didn't simply stuff my bloody clothes in the bag and throw it back in the Dumpster. I braved the smell once more, and buried the bag with the clothes deep beneath the garbage.

But I kept the knife.

The most incriminating piece of evidence.

I didn't know why.

1666 Red Coach Lane. Here I come. The map was a big help. Go down two blocks and turn right at the light. Then make a left and drive to the end of the cul-de-sac. I didn't live that far from the supermarket. Nothing in Carlsrue was far from anything else, though. The police station was probably just around the block. I probably knew half the cops.

My house was on the left. It could have been a base on the moon it looked so unfamiliar.

Still, I parked in the driveway and walked up to the door.

It was hard not to knock.

My mother had left the light on, but fortunately she had gone to bed. I stepped inside and quickly closed the door. The sooner I got to bed the better. I had gone out in one set of clothes, but was returning in another set. If my mom saw me, there'd be questions. I left the knife in the trunk of the car, hidden beneath the spare tire. Someone would have to look for it to find it.

I had a small problem.

I didn't know which bedroom was mine.

At the first door, I stood and listened closely. Soft snoring inside.

I tried door number two. No sound. I opened the door carefully. A shaft of light from the living room landed on the face of a sleeping seven- or eight-year-old boy. Before I could close the door, the boy's eyes popped open.

"What?" he mumbled.

"It's just me," I whispered loudly. "Go back to sleep."

The boy sat up. His hair was light blond; he

had the face of a mischievous angel. He rubbed his sleepy blue eyes. "What time is it?" he asked.

"Late. Go back to sleep."

"Why did you open my door?"

"It was an accident. Go back to sleep."

"I want a glass of water."

I hesitated, glancing at the door where the snoring was. My room must be the one at the end of the hall. Unless there were more kids in this family. For all I knew, I shared a room with a sister.

"I'll get you a glass of water," I said.

The boy threw off his blankets. "I want a doughnut."

"What? At three in the morning?"

He climbed out of bed. He wore *Star Wars* pajamas. I knew about the movies, although I couldn't remember having seen them. My brother was a four-foot-tall Jedi knight. He staggered over to me, still rubbing his eyes.

"Mom said I could have a doughnut after dinner, but I didn't eat it," he explained. "I want it now." He added, "Would you like one?"

Door number one was still snoring. "OK," I said.

Minutes later we sat at the kitchen table eating doughnuts and drinking milk. Hopefully the rush of sugar would stimulate my memory. My little brother was absolutely adorable. The way he ate his doughnut—it was as if the dessert were a holy sacrament. His hair constantly fell into his eyes, and when he took a drink of milk, half of it ended up as a mustache on his face. A pity I couldn't remember his name.

"Where were you?" he asked.

"Oh, I was just out cruising around."

"With Mitch?"

"No." Did I have a boyfriend? Was he cute? "I was alone."

"Why were you out so late?"

"I don't know. I just was. What did you do tonight?"

He shrugged. "Watched TV. Do you know Clyde on that new show about robots? He died tonight."

"How did he die?"

My brother's eyes widened. "He got struck with lightning. It was real cool. For a few minutes it looked like his positronic brain was going to melt." He stuffed another bite in his mouth. "But they might fix him next week."

"You never know with robots," I agreed.

"Crystal's mom called. She was looking for Crystal."

"Oh."

"Did you see her?"

"No."

"I thought you were going over to her house?"

"I changed my mind," I said.

"I like Crystal. Can I come to her birthday party?"

"I don't see why not."

"But isn't it just going to be for people in high school and stuff?"

"Maybe. Let me ask her."

My brother was confused. "How can you ask her? I thought it was going to be a surprise party."

"You're right. We won't ask her. But you just come. I'm sure she won't mind."

My little brother stared at me with his perfect blue eyes. "Are you OK, Jen?"

I forced a smile. "Sure. Don't I seem OK?"

"Your voice sounds funny."

"I'm just tired." I gestured to the box of doughnuts. "Would you like another one?"

He was interested. "You won't tell Mom?"

"No." I paused. "How's Mom?"

He grabbed the doughnut. "Fine."

"That's good. How's Dad?"

My little brother set the doughnut down.

He looked at me as if I'd lost my mind.

"Dad's dead," he said. "He died five years ago."

I didn't know what to say.

* * *

The last door on the right was to a bedroom that belonged to me, alone. There was a poster of the Swiss Alps on one wall, a picture of an Australian coral reef on the other. Maybe I liked to travel. I had a lot of books, tons of CDs. If I'd been less tired, I would have rummaged through the room and searched for clues to my identity. But I was exhausted and wanted to wash again before I got into bed. I may have washed off enough blood to get by at Denny's late at night, but I couldn't get a trace of blood on my sheet. Fortunately, I had my own bathroom.

The hot shower was delicious. I shampooed my hair three times.

I bandaged the cuts on my hand. The deep one continued to sting.

I was in bed only ten seconds when I started to doze.

I hoped, when I woke up, that I would remember everything.

My last thought was of the dead girl. Her empty eyes.

I wondered what her last thoughts had been.

Yet not all thoughts come in waking.

Not all memory is tied to the world.

In a dream I could never have made up, I sat late at night beside a wide river and smoked a drug that was as potent as it was sweet. The clouds of the intoxicant whirled around my head like mental vapors that had seeped from my ears. It was as if my mind flew out with each exhalation of the sticky smoke. I was not merely stoned. Because a stoned person did not continue to get higher and higher as I did. Leaning my head back and staring up at the stars, I knew that before the night was over I would touch them.

Then the scene changed. The river vanished.

I sat before an old woman. Her face was dark and lined, and she wore a black veil that partially hid her eyes—such bitterness was revealed by those eyes. The expression in them was sharper than a snake's bite. On the wooden table between us lay a stack of cards. She asked me to lift them, to touch them, breathe on them even. Then she took them and spread them out, her bony hands shaking as she did so. One by one she turned them over. Tarot cards.

The Death card came first. It didn't matter how many times I shuffled the deck. It was always first. But that didn't bother me. In fact, it made me laugh, so hard I actually felt as if my guts would spill out on to the table. I knew the old woman would like to take a dagger to me, if she dared. We were not friends. But she had something I wanted and intended to get. What I had, however, that she could possibly want was not clear.

The cards made me laugh, but they didn't satisfy me. Gesturing angrily, I insisted she continue on to the next step. She shook her head—there was fear in her eyes. She stood to leave, and told me to do likewise. It was then I grabbed her and pulled a knife on her. Perhaps what I possessed of hers was her very life. Forcing her wrist down on top of the Death card, I grinned and ran the blade lightly over her upturned palm. The blood trickled onto the grim Tarot card. I began to laugh again. Everything seemed so funny. I could do whatever I wanted and no one could stop me.

I knew then that I was the most powerful creature in the world.

CHAPTER 3

───✦───

THE FIRST THING I SAW IN THE MORNING WAS MY mother's face. But I only knew it was my mother through deduction. As far as I could tell, I'd never seen the woman before in my life. She stuck her head in through my door. An attractive woman in her early forties, she wore a smart plaid suit and carried a briefcase in her right hand. I summed her up quickly. A businesswoman, already late for an appointment. Her hair was the color of mine but she had my brother's eyes. She appeared annoyed with me, but not angry. I wondered if I was a good daughter.

"Are you getting up today?" she asked.

I sat up. "Damn," I muttered. I still didn't know who I was.

"Tired? That will teach you to stay out so late. Where were you anyway?"

I rubbed my head. "I don't remember." Naturally I lied. All I could remember *was* last night —and my nightmare, of course. How fitting that I should be having dreams about stabbing fortune-tellers. My mother came farther into the room and picked up the shoes I had worn the previous night. They were still muddy. I had to remember to clean them. My mother put them in the corner, out of the way.

"It looks like you were hiking in the woods," she said.

"That's not true."

My mother stood with her hands on her hips. "You were out with Mitch."

"Well."

She smiled because she thought she'd got me. "You don't have to tell me. I still remember what it was like to be a teenager. As long as you're home safe. Oh, I told you Crystal's mom called. Do you know if she got home OK?"

I nodded. "She's fine."

"You saw her after you called me?"

I hesitated. One lie made the next lie that more difficult. "Yeah, she's fine."

"That's a relief. Can you take Ken to school? I'm running late."

I swung my legs over the side of the bed. "No problem."

My mother squinted at my right hand. "You cut yourself?"

"Yeah, last night." The deeper cut continued to ache slightly.

"How did you do it?"

"On a broken glass."

"Do you want me to look at the cuts?"

"It's not necessary. They're more like scratches."

My mother hesitated. "Are you working tonight?"

"Yeah."

"When?"

"The late shift—I think. But I'm not sure."

"If you're going to be here, cancel the babysitter for Ken. Call me at the clinic."

The clinic? Maybe she was a doctor or nurse. "I will," I promised.

Before I left the house, I was going to have to find my phone book.

In the kitchen, Ken, my little brother, was eating a bowl of corn flakes, at least two cups too much for him. He looked up as I entered. I was still in the sweats I had taken from the trunk of the Celica. Examining them in my room before going to bed, I had not found a single trace of blood on them.

"Good morning, Jen," he said with a full mouth.

"Good morning, Ken," I replied.

Another mistake. "Are you going to call me Ken now?" He looked disappointed.

I sat down at the table. "What would you like me to call you?"

"What you always call me."

I forced a laugh. "I've forgotten what that is."

He went back to his cereal. "Yeah, right. You've been calling me Gator since I grew teeth."

"Do you know why I call you Gator?"

"Of course. I used to bite you when I was small."

This time I laughed spontaneously. Maybe I hadn't forgotten everything. I had just met this kid. I knew nothing about him, except that he liked doughnuts, milk, and corn flakes. Yet I felt such profound affection for him. I couldn't explain it. Maybe love survives when memory fails.

Driving Gator to his school, I ran into a major difficulty. I didn't know where it was. For that matter, I didn't know where my own school was. Sitting patiently beside me, Gator seemed perplexed at my choice of turns. A brilliant idea came to me.

"Hey, Gator," I said. "How would you like to drive?"

He made a face. "I can't drive. I don't have a license."

"You don't need a license to steer. How about you sit on my lap and turn the steering wheel while I take care of the brake and gas pedal?"

He was excited. "You won't tell Mom?"

"No way. It's my idea. Here, let me pull over and rearrange my seat belt so that it holds both of us."

"Cool," Gator said.

A few minutes later Gator was sitting on my lap, having the time of his life. I told him to swing by my school first, just to show all the big kids what an expert driver he was. So I got a good look at Carlsrue High. Gator honked as he went by the school.

"I'm doing pretty good, huh?" he said.

"You're great," I said. Actually, I was having to help him turn the wheel a bit. But my brother sure knew his way around. He even took a short cut to his elementary school. As we parked and he got out, he stopped to hug me.

"Can I drive tomorrow?" he asked.

I messed up his blond hair. "We'll see. Have fun today."

"You, too." He paused as he let go of me. "Jen?"

"Yes?"

"Your voice still sounds kind of funny."

I realized what he was referring to. Even if I had the same vocal cords as I'd had yesterday, in the same throat, my personality was not the same. And personality greatly affects the quality of a voice. I needed more tapes of Jennifer Hobbs's voice, besides the one on my answering machine. I poked Gator in the stomach.

"That's because I'm not really your sister. I'm a robot."

He thought that was funny. "Don't get struck by lightning."

His remark made me quiet. Something must have struck me, hard, to make me lose my identity. "I'll try not to," I told him.

Carlsrue High was larger than I would have expected, judging by the size of the town. It was located at the edge of the city, bordered on two sides by the same huge tract of woods where I had awakened the previous night. Yet the school wasn't really that close to the pond. It was still six miles away. I believe that the sight of the woods would have been more relaxing if I hadn't known there was a body lying in them, unattended. Images of bugs and animals crawling over the girl's face continued to haunt me. I didn't know how long I could go without notifying the police.

Why was I stalling?

Why didn't I just confess my amnesia?

Well, I kept thinking my memory would return any second. It seemed inconceivable that it could be gone forever. Also, now that I had already distorted the evidence, I seemed to be guilty. I even *felt* guilty. Finally, I doubted anyone would believe I had lost all my memory. I knew that total amnesia was rare, except in cases of serious brain damage. Of course I had no idea how I knew this. I couldn't remember the book I had read it in.

After parking my Celica in the lot in the back, I walked toward the campus.

I wondered what I had first period.

I was about fifty feet into the school when someone called my name. I had barely turned to a big, cute jock when he had his arms around me and his lips pressed against mine.

"Jenny," he said. Then he was kissing me.

I kissed him back—what the hell.

When we were done he took a step back and checked me out. I did likewise—I was really curious about my taste in boys. The guy was built; he looked like a quarterback in his letter-man jacket with his cocky swagger. His green eyes and tousled brown hair were his best features. Yet his face was somewhat flattened. He looked as if he had run into a goal post or two in his athletic career. I wasn't sure if I liked him or not, but I figured I was probably sleeping with him. God, maybe I was in love with him. I didn't know. He seemed to be waiting for me to say something, but I just smiled. I was pretty sure I was looking at Mitch.

"What's wrong, Jenny?" he asked.

"Nothing. How are you doing?"

"Great." He looked around and lowered his voice. "Did you bring the money?"

I still only had twenty-five dollars or so in my purse. "Ah, how much do you need?"

"Three hundred. We went over this yesterday a dozen times."

"I don't have it on me right now. Can I give it to you later?"

His face flushed an angry red. "Jenny, I need that money this afternoon. Duke is sending his guys for it."

"Can Duke get it tomorrow?"

Mitch was mad. "No! I've put them off for two weeks. If I don't give it to them today, they'll break one of my thumbs. Tomorrow they break the other one." He was beside himself. "How could you just forget it? You know what this means to me."

"I just forgot." That was the understatement of the year.

"Do you have it at home? Can I swing by and get it?"

"I think it's there. Why don't you give me a call later."

"But you go into work at two, don't you?"

"Yeah, but I'll go home first." From my license I knew I was eighteen years old. From that and Mitch's comments, I figured I must be a senior on a half-day schedule. I wondered where I worked. And what I was doing with a boyfriend who owed money to loan sharks. I added, "Can we write Duke a check?"

Mitch shook his head like, well, I'd lost my mind. "No. Duke doesn't take checks. He doesn't pay tax. He works in cash, or pain. Nothing else."

"Sounds like a nice guy," I remarked.

"Jenny, I don't understand your attitude."

That made two of us. "I'll try to get you the money later. That's all I can say." I paused. "Hey, can you do me a favor?"

He continued to fume, clasping and unclasping his hands. He was probably thinking what it would feel like to have them in a cast. "What?" he grumbled.

"Could you walk me to class today?" I asked. "To each class?"

"Why?"

"I thought it would be romantic."

"I'm about to have bones broken and you're talking about romance."

"If you walk me to each of my classes, I might have an easier time finding the money." I just hoped it was at home, in a shoe box or something. Maybe I could borrow it from Gator's piggy bank. I had a feeling that kid would do anything for his big sister.

Mitch walked me to Jennifer Hobbs's first period, which turned out to be psychology. The teacher was a thirty-year-old woman in a miniskirt so short that it explained why eighty percent of the class was male. I sat in the back and tried to look inconspicuous. The topic of the day was peer group pressure. I was the first person the teacher addressed.

"Do you no longer like the front of the room, Jenny?" she asked.

I shrugged. "I decided to give someone else a chance at the best seat."

"Do you personally feel the effect of peer pressure on you each day?"

"No."

"Not at all?"

"No." Keep it simple and stupid. The teacher went on to somebody else—I was safe for another hour.

Mitch walked me to second period, grumbling the whole way about Duke's boys and their propensity for violence. This class turned out to be more difficult. It was chemistry and I had no textbook with me, no lab manual. I had not seen them in my bedroom that morning. They must be in my locker, I decided. The teacher, a gray

lizard of a man, noticed I had brought no sup-
plies and wanted to know what was up. I just
shrugged. It didn't work with this guy.

"Were you thinking of sleeping in class today,
Jenny?" he asked.

"I just forgot my books, is all."

When he frowned the liver spots on his forehead bunched together to form the shape of the
State of Texas. "Where's your lab partner?"

"I don't know."

"Is she at school today?"

"I don't know."

The teacher sighed. "I find it hard to believe
you don't know where Crystal is. I don't think
I've ever seen you two apart."

"Well, we don't sleep together."

Fortunately, Mr. Ugly had a sense of humor.
He smiled crookedly. "Borrow a pen and some
paper from somebody. We'll be taking a lot of
notes today." He added, "And, Jenny?"

"Yes, sir?"

"Make a copy of your notes for Crystal. Give
them to her this evening. There'll be a quiz
tomorrow."

"OK."

Nothing was OK. My mind was racing.

Crystal was not at school.

Crystal had not come home last night.

I never went anywhere without Crystal.

Third and fourth period would have to wait until tomorrow, if I ever did return to school. When chemistry was over, I rushed to my car without waiting for Mitch. I drove home at high speed. That morning, I'd been in too much of a hurry getting Gator and myself to school to examine my room. Now I was going to take the time.

Yet it didn't take me long to find what I needed—a yearbook. Last year's annual. I opened to the junior pictures, found myself. Nice smile, bad hair day. Crystal—I didn't even know her last name. I had to start with Frank Adams, Julie Astra . . . Maybe there would be more than one Crystal.

But there was only one. Crystal Denger.

She had such beautiful blue eyes, blond hair.

I had seen both last night, covered with blood.

My best friend.

CHAPTER 4

FOR THE FIRST TIME SINCE WAKING UP BESIDE THE pond, I cried. Not the solitary tear I had shed over Crystal's body, but huge gushing sobs. They poured out of me. The fact that I didn't know who I was crying for didn't lessen my pain. Ironically, it made it worse. Because I could not mourn her properly with my special memories of her. Deep in my chest, I felt only a huge void, a black hole into which all gentle images had been consumed. For ten minutes straight, I wept. When I looked down at Crystal's picture, it was smeared with my tears. It was as if I were viewing her underwater, as if someone had sunk her body to the floor of the pond. Right then, I swore, I wouldn't rest until her murderer was found.

"I have to call the police," I said out loud. "I have to lead them to her body. I have to give them the knife."

I reached for the phone.

Something stopped me. Maybe it was the blinking light on my answering machine. There were four messages, displayed in digital. Two were from last night, two from this morning. The first three were from Crystal's mother. Each sounded more desperate than the last. Please call me and let me know where Crystal is. The fourth was from a guy. His voice was deep, soothing. He had an accent, maybe Middle Eastern.

"Hello, Jenny. This is Amir. I have to talk to you about last night. Please call me as soon as you can. Thanks."

He'd hung up without leaving a phone number. Recalling my earlier vow, I went searching for my "little black book." Surprisingly it was black and little when I found it lying facedown on my desktop. By chance, if it was chance, the page was open to *A*. Amir was listed. He obviously did not have a last name in my universe. Taking a few deep breaths, I sat down and dialed his number. He answered on the first ring, as if he had been waiting by the phone for me to call.

"Hello?"

"Hi, this is Jenny."

He paused. "You got my message."

"Yes."

"What's wrong?"

"Nothing."

"You sound out of breath." He was definitely from the Middle East.

"I'm fine." I paused. "Why do you want to talk about last night?"

"You should know." He paused. "Are you at school?"

"No. I wasn't feeling well. I took the day off."

"Have you spoken to Crystal today?"

"No." This must be her boyfriend, I thought.

"This morning I got a call from her mother. She says Crystal never came home last night. Do you know where she is?"

"No."

"She hasn't contacted you?"

"No, I said."

Amir drew in a deep breath. "Where the hell could she be?"

I didn't know who the hell Amir was. "I have no idea."

"Can I come over? We need to talk."

I hesitated. It sounded as if I'd seen Amir last night. Perhaps he would be a good place to start to pick up the pieces of my life.

"Come now," I said.

* * *

He couldn't have lived far away. Then again, I reminded myself, nothing in Carlsrue was more than three miles from anything else. I was hardly off the phone when he was at my door. He came in without being invited.

If Mitch was flat, Amir was exotic. There was an intensity to him that convinced me I'd have to move carefully around him if I wished to keep my lost memory secret. Approximately twenty, he had the dark skin of someone who had grown up in deep desert. Everything about his face was sharp and pointy except his eyelids, his lips—these were heavy and full. He had a raw sensual bearing. His style was smooth—he moved slowly like a lion with untapped power ready to burst out at a moment's notice. He had sat down on the couch before I closed the front door. I took the chair across from him. He was clearly worried.

"I called Crystal's mother just before coming here," he said. "Crystal still hasn't shown up. You better call her mother soon. Also, she's contacted the police. They might swing by at any minute." He paused. "Your eyes are red. You've been crying."

I shrugged. It was becoming my most common gesture.

"I'm just worried about her," I said.

He leaned forward. "You really don't know where she is?"

"No."

"You were with her last. How was she when you left her?"

I fidgeted. "OK."

"She wasn't upset?"

"No." Why should she be upset?

"Where did you two go after you left my house?"

"I—I took her home."

"But her mother says she never came home." He paused. "Did you go to Mitch's house?"

"I— No."

"Where did you go?"

"I told you, I took her home."

He sighed and sat back on the sofa. "Jenny, the time for games is past. We both know Crystal was upset last night. If she's run away, we're going to have to tell her mother why. We're probably going to have to tell the police."

I stopped and stared at him. "Why would she run away?"

He snorted. "Isn't it obvious?"

I spoke carefully. "Not necessarily. Explain it to me."

Amir looked out the window. In profile, his face was remarkably handsome. He looked like a young god, but with earthly appetites. His features seemed to sag as he contemplated my question.

"You know she suspected we were having an affair," he said finally.

"Really?" I was astounded. But was it true? God, this was awful, not knowing who I had slept with, and whether I had enjoyed myself or not. I added carefully, "How would she suspect that?"

Amir lowered his head. "She just had to follow my eyes."

I took a chance. "I didn't say anything to her."

He looked up. "Are you sure? When you two left my place, I thought you were going to tell her."

"I swear, I can't remember saying a thing to her."

He appeared relieved. We must have done the dirty deed. Oh wow. Mitch and Amir in the same week. At least I wasn't boring. But then Amir's face clouded over again.

"Then why would she run away?" he asked.

"We're not sure she ran away."

"Of course she did. She didn't just disappear from the planet." He frowned. "Her mother says her car is still in the driveway. Isn't that odd?"

"Yeah." I must have driven her to the woods. That fact did not reassure me. Amir was staring at me again. He looked as if he wished I were close enough to touch, to comfort.

"I feel terrible about what happened," he said finally.

"So do I."

"I didn't plan it."

"No. It wasn't planned."

"That night . . . I just felt so close to you."

"We don't have to talk about it."

He smiled faintly. "But I don't totally regret it. I think it was one of those things, you know, that was destined to happen."

It was remarkable that he could weave destiny and cheating on my best friend—and his girlfriend—together to make it sound not only believable, but honorable. His voice was still gentle, seductive. I could envision him as a stage hypnotist, working a smoked-filled tavern in Cairo. "Now you see it, now you don't." Yet there was also something endearing about him. It was funny, but he was the first person I found to be familiar. Or maybe it wasn't so funny since we'd been having sex recently. Where the mind fails, the senses remember. I realized he was waiting for me to respond.

"I suppose," I added hastily. "But I don't think it's going to happen again."

His smile broadened. "Who would have thought it would happen the first time?" A pause. "Did you?"

"No."

"That's not what you said at the time."

I looked away. This was too weird, with Crystal

already dead and all. In his defense, however, he didn't know that.

"I can't remember what I said," I replied.

He took the hint and returned to being the worried boyfriend.

"If she did leave town," he said, "then someone gave her a ride. At least to the bus station. Any possible candidates?"

"I can't think of anyone offhand."

"What about Debra Ruso?"

"She wouldn't do it."

"What about Cindy Taylor?"

"I don't know. Look, what's the point of this? When she wants to call, she will. Until then—we can only wait."

Amir studied me. "What if something's happened to her?"

It was my turn to lower my head. "Nothing's happened to her."

Amir left a few minutes later. He promised to stay in touch. I didn't kiss him goodbye, although I think he expected it. I watched as he pulled away in his old white Ford. He obviously didn't have much money. Still, there was something about him. Inside me, he was not a blank slate. Whatever mark he had made there, it must have been pretty deep.

I had to call Crystal's mother, but I knew I

couldn't lie to her. Nor could I tell her that her daughter was dead. The charade had to end, at least a portion of it. The phone was close by. I just had to dial 911 to pour my heart out. Yet I knew they taped 911 calls. Whatever I said, it would be forever. All the way to court, to the gas chamber. Then again, I didn't know if Oregon had the death penalty.

I probably hadn't known last week either.

I picked up the phone, put a couch pillow half over my mouth. 911 it would be. A sharp-voiced woman answered.

"Hello, Carlsrue Police Station. What is the nature of your emergency?"

I forced my voice down, deep and husky. "There is a body of a young woman by a pond one mile east of Highway Seventeen. Her name is Crystal Denger. This is not a crank call."

I hung up.

At least now the bugs would no longer disturb Crystal.

CHAPTER 5

THE POLICE WOULDN'T TAKE LONG TO FIND THE body. They'd take even less time to reach my door. Jennifer Hobbs would be a prime candidate—Crystal's best friend, the last one to see the victim alive. Before they arrived, I had to get rid of the knife. They probably wouldn't buy my story because it was so lame. I tried to remember all the things I'd told people since I got up so I wouldn't contradict myself. Keep it simple and stupid, I reminded myself again. The latter part would come naturally.

I drove down the block to a local park and hid the knife under a bush, covering it with a foot of moist dirt and leaves. I got a crick in my neck checking to make sure no one was watching. I felt so guilty, and I had done nothing wrong. Almost nothing. I wondered what Crystal had been like. Why I would have betrayed her. Amir was sexy, a smooth operator. But what else did he have that I'd stab my best friend in the back to get?

Cancel that thought. I had not stabbed anyone.

It was twelve-thirty when I got back to my house.

At two-fifteen Denny's called and asked where I was. No wonder Elaine hadn't given me a menu—I worked at Denny's. I told them I was feeling sick and got off the line before they could argue with me.

At two-twenty Mitch called.

"Why aren't you at work?" he asked. "Why did you leave school?"

"I don't feel good."

"Do you have the money?"

Not, "You poor dear."

"I don't know. I have to look. Can't you stall Duke's boys until tomorrow?"

He was exasperated. "You stall these guys at a price. Can't you just go to the bank?"

"I'll try."

"When should I come over?"

"I don't know. Later."

He paused. "What's wrong?"

"Nothing."

"You sound funny."

"I'm fine. I mean, I'm sick. Look, I've got to go."

"Have you seen Crystal? People are saying she's missing."

"No. But I'm sure she'll turn up."

The police arrived at three-fifteen. By then Gator was home. Fortunately he took the bus in the afternoon, and didn't rely on his senile chauffeur. He was playing a video game in the living room when the knock came at the door. I told him to go to his room.

"Why?" he asked.

"Just do what I say," I snapped.

Gator wasn't used to a sister with a sharp tongue. He fled. Opening the front door, I felt as if I were stepping in front of a firing squad. I had seen the black and whites pull up, and wondered now if I would be leaving in one of them.

There were two cops in uniform, one plainclothes officer. The latter was no doubt a detective. In his midfifties, he looked kindly. Over the years, the deep lines of his face seemed to have been dug into his soft flesh from sympathy rather than age. He had a twinkle in his gray eyes that he probably used to good advantage when he was interrogating suspects. His shoes were expensive, his coat well tailored. He introduced himself as Lieutenant Harvey Lott and asked if I was Jennifer Hobbs.

"Yes, I'm Jenny." Pretty sure I am.

He gestured. "These are my two associates, Officer Gallager and Officer Jakes. May we come in?"

"Sure." I stepped aside. Gator's toys lay about. "Please excuse the mess."

"Hi, Jenny," the youngest cop said to me as he stepped by. Officer Jakes. He knew me, liked me. Probably didn't know I cheated on my best friend. His dark hair was cut short like a marine's, but he had a cute face and wasn't much older than me.

"How are you doing?" I asked.

Jakes sighed. "Not so good."

They had come to tell me that my best friend was dead. I was not supposed to know that. I had to remember that. My shock would have to be replayed, not that that would be difficult. Just having so many cops in my living room made me feel like fainting. I wondered if Gator had eaten all the doughnuts, if I could make them go away if I filled their bellies with Hostess. I doubted it.

"What's this about?" I asked.

"May we sit down?" Lt. Lott asked.

"Sure," I said.

They took the couch, all three of them. They posed a formidable front. Lt. Lott gestured for me to take the chair across from them. "Please," he said.

I sat down. "Is something the matter?" I asked.

Lt. Lott's expression was unhappy. "Yes, I'm afraid there is. A couple of hours ago our office received an anonymous call. It directed us to search the woods a mile east of Highway Seventeen." Lt. Lott paused. He was feeling me out. Already, I was a suspect.

"For what?" I asked innocently.

"A body," he said flatly.

"Oh."

Lt. Lott took a breath. "This is very difficult. We found a body. It belongs to a young woman we understand is your best friend. Crystal Denger."

I just stared at them. I didn't have to act. To have the reality spoken aloud was painful enough. "What?" I asked.

Officer Jakes spoke up. "It's Crystal, Jenny." His voice was pained. "We're sorry to have to tell you."

I swallowed. "Are you sure it's Crystal?"

Jakes nodded. "It's her. I could ID the body myself."

I put my hand to my head. "Oh God."

"We realize this must be terribly painful for you," Lt. Lott said.

I nodded weakly. "Yes."

Officer Jakes spoke gently. "If you're up to it, Jenny, we'd like to ask you some questions." He added, "We have to catch the guy who did this. Quick."

"I understand," I mumbled.

"How old are you, Jenny?" Lt. Lott asked.

"Eighteen."

"Legally, in this state, that makes you an adult," Lt. Lott continued. "But if you would prefer to wait to have your parents present, we can hold off on our questions. You might even want a lawyer present."

I acted shocked. I was shocked. "I don't need a lawyer."

"Would you like your parents present?" Lt. Lott repeated.

"There's just my mom. No, I can answer your questions."

"We understand you were the last one to see Crystal?" Lt. Lott said.

I nodded. "I saw her last night."

Lt. Lott took out a small notepad. "Could you start at the beginning of the evening? Where you were? What you were doing?"

I shrugged. "Crystal and I—we were with Amir. That's Crystal's boyfriend."

"What's Amir's last name?"

"I don't know. It's some Middle Eastern name."

"You were at his place?" Lt. Lott asked.

"Yes."

"How long were you there? During what time period?"

My eyes moistened. "I can't remember exactly."

Officer Jakes spoke quickly. "Can I get you a glass of water? A tissue?"

"I'm fine," I whispered. This was it. I was going to have to invent every detail, and then later get contradicted by everybody else. My only hope was to be vague. But I had a feeling that wouldn't get very far with Lt. Lott. He had a pleasant personality, but I could see he was sharp. He cast Officer Jakes a hard look, as if to say shut up and let me question the girl. Then the detective turned back to me, his pen ready.

"Can you give me a rough idea of the time you were at Amir's house?" he asked.

"Between nine and eleven."

"What were you doing there?"

"Just hanging out."

"Could you be more specific?"

"Well, we watched TV, listened to music, ate."

"What did you eat?"

"Pardon?"

"Did you eat food from his refrigerator? Or did you order out?"

I hesitated. "I can't remember."

"You have no idea what you ate?"

"No."

"But you didn't come and go? You stayed at Amir's the whole time?"

"Yes."

"Until eleven o'clock?"

"It could have been later."

"How late? Until twelve o'clock?"

"Possibly."

"Then what did you do?"

"I took Crystal home."

The detective glanced at the other cops. "You're sure you took her straight home?"

"Yes."

"Did you stay long enough to see her go in the house?"

"No."

"You dropped her at the end of the driveway? At the curb?"

"Yes."

"Then you drove away?"

"Yes."

"Where did you go next?"

"I came home. But I didn't go inside. I decided to go for a walk."

"In the middle of the night?"

"I sometimes go for walks late at night."

"Did you see anyone while you were on this walk?"

"No."

"How long did you walk?"

"I don't know."

' Approximately?"

I shrugged. "An hour."

"You walked for an hour around Carlsrue in the middle of the night?"

"It could have been less."

"Did you have a watch on during this time?"

"No."

"Do you usually wear a watch?"

"Sometimes I do. Sometimes I don't."

"What time did you return home?"

"I came back around one, maybe a little later."

"Then you came in and went to bed?"

"No."

Detective Lott paused. "Did you go back out?"

"Yes. I went to Denny's."

"Why?"

"I was hungry."

"Did you drive there?"

"Yes."

"Did you eat there?"

"Yes. Apple pie and coffee."

"Did you talk to anyone there?"

"Yes. Elaine. She's a waitress there."

"Do you work?"

"Yes. At the same Denny's."

"Do you often go to Denny's so late at night?"

"No."

"What was special about last night?"

"I told you, I was hungry."

"How long did you stay at Denny's?"

"I don't know. An hour maybe."

"So you left there about two?"

"I think it was closer to three."

"But you said you went there about one. Did you stay two hours?"

"Like I said, I'm not sure about any of these times. I didn't have a watch on. It may be that I didn't get there until two in the morning."

Lt. Lott paused to take a deep breath. He studied his notes. "An hour here or there is important. *When* you last saw Crystal is absolutely crucial. We have to narrow down the time when she was killed."

"Can't the coroner do that?"

"Crystal's body was lying in the woods for maybe twelve hours. After so long a period, it's

impossible to pinpoint the exact time of death."
He paused. "We could really use your help here."

You're not the only one, I thought. "I'm trying
to remember as best I can." I gestured helplessly.
"This is such a shock."

Lt. Lott nodded sympathetically. "To lose a
best friend is not easy." He paused. "Tell me a
little about your relationship with Crystal?"

"You just said it. We were best friends."

"I understand. But best friends have all kinds
of relationships. Did you compete with each
other?"

"No."

"At school? With guys?"

"No."

"How long had she been going with Amir?"

I paused. "It's hard to say exactly when they
started dating. A few months."

"Do you have a boyfriend?"

"Yes."

"What's his name?"

"Mitch."

Lt. Lott made a note. "Mitch what?"

"Pardon?"

"What's his last name?"

I paused. "That's funny, I can't remember
right now."

That raised a stir. "You don't know your
boyfriend's last name?" Lt. Lott asked.

"It's Severs," Officer Jakes said. "He's Carlsrue High's quarterback."

Lt. Lott was annoyed at the volunteered information. "Thank you, Officer, I would appreciate if you would allow Jenny to answer the questions." The detective returned to me. "How could you forget your boyfriend's last name?"

"I don't know."

"Do you often have trouble with your memory?"

"No."

"Do you take drugs?"

"Pardon?"

"Pot? Cocaine? Speed? Don't worry, we won't hold it against you."

"I don't do drugs."

"Did Crystal?"

"No."

"Does Amir?"

"He's never done them around me."

"Does Mitch?"

"No."

"Does he gamble?"

"Who?"

"Mitch."

"Not that I know of. Why?"

"Just wondering." Lt. Lott was writing away. "How long have you been going out with Mitch?"

"A few months."

"Could you be more specific?"

"I've known him for years. It's hard to say exactly when we started dating. We hung out together before we started going out."

"How would you characterize your relationship with Mitch?"

"It's good."

"Did Crystal approve of your relationship with Mitch?"

"Yes."

"Did you approve of Crystal's relationship with Amir?"

"Yes. He's a nice guy. Have you talked to him yet?"

"We'll be talking to him soon." Lt. Lott paused. "What is your relationship with Amir?"

I shrugged. "He's my friend."

"Did the four of you often do things together?"

"Sometimes."

"Seldom? Often?"

"Just sometimes."

"Were there any arguments among the four of you?"

"No. I mean, sometimes we argued. Everybody argues."

"Did Amir like Mitch?"

"I suppose."

"Did Mitch like Amir?"

"I think so."

"Did you, or Crystal, or Amir argue last night?"

I remembered what Amir had said about Crystal's being upset. "No. But Crystal was in a bad mood."

"Why?"

"I don't know."

"Did she often get in bad moods?"

"No."

"Did anything happen last night, anything at all, to upset her?"

"No."

Lt. Lott sighed and studied his notes again. "The time you dropped Crystal off at home still confuses me. Was it eleven o'clock? Twelve o'clock? One o'clock?"

"Twelve is my best guess."

"Then if you got to the Denny's at two, you must have walked for two hours."

I remembered I got to Denny's at two-fifteen. But did Elaine remember? I hoped not. "I may have got to Denny's closer to one. I'm just not sure."

"When Crystal got out of your car, was she in a bad mood?"

"Sort of."

"What 'sort of' things was she saying that made you think she was upset?"

"It was nothing specific. She was just quiet."

"Was she mad at Amir?"

"I don't think so."

"At you?"

"No."

"She just didn't feel good?"

"I suppose."

"Jenny, here I want you to stop and remember as best you can. When you dropped Crystal off, did you see her walk toward her front door?"

I hesitated. "I didn't look. She got out of the car and I drove away."

"Have you spoken to her mother since then?"

"No."

"But she called here several times looking for Crystal. Why didn't you call her back?"

"I didn't know she called." I added, "My answering machine was on. I didn't check my messages."

"Have you checked them at all today?"

I hesitated. "Yes. Just before you got here."

"You left school early today. Why was that?"

Lt. Lott had found out a lot quickly. "I wasn't feeling well," I replied.

"You weren't upset about anything?"

"No."

"You didn't know Crystal was dead, did you?"

Officer Jakes interrupted. "Lieutenant, I think that question is completely out of line. These two girls grew up together. To imply that Jenny is responsible for Crystal's murder is just—"

"Officer Jakes," Lt. Lott interrupted firmly. "I will complete my questioning of Jenny with you outside, waiting in the squad car. That is all. Dismissed."

Officer Jakes scowled at the detective as he stood. But he spoke to me. "I'm sorry about Crystal, Jenny."

I nodded weakly. "So am I. Thanks for your support."

When Jakes was gone, Lott resumed his questioning.

"Did you suspect, when you were at school this morning, that something had happened to Crystal?" he asked.

"No."

"Is it your habit not to check your messages in the morning?"

"I sometimes go for a long time without checking them." I paused. "May I ask a question, Lieutenant?"

"Yes, please," Lt. Lott said.

"Am I a suspect in Crystal's murder?"

The detective was smooth. "We have no suspects at this point. All we have is a body." He paused. "We don't even have a murder weapon."

I paused. "How did she die?"

"She was stabbed to death."

I lowered my head. "Poor Crystal."

"We don't know how she came to be in the woods late at night," Lt. Lott went on. "We do know she didn't drive herself there. Her car is still parked in front of her house."

"I see."

"But there are fresh tire tracks not far from the pond where we found Crystal. They're in the dirt, at the side of Highway Seventeen. There are also footprints around the body, prints that don't belong to Crystal. From their size, they appear to belong to a woman."

"There's only one set of footprints, other than Crystal's?" I asked.

Lt. Lott stared me straight in the eye. His interrogation had led to this point, I knew. "Can you keep this information confidential?" he asked.

"Yes."

"The answer is, yes. It would appear that Crystal was stabbed to death by a female, or else a very small man." Lt. Lott added casually, nodding at my feet, "Those shoes you have on now. Were you wearing them last night?"

I had on different shoes than I'd had on last night. The others were still a bit muddy— perhaps, I worried, a bit bloody. Both sets of shoes were Nikes. My eyes involuntarily strayed in the direction of my bedroom and I had to force them back and meet the detective's stare. I had to fight to remain calm.

I was the only one with her last night! I must have— No!

"Yes," I said. "Would you like to look at them?"

He was way ahead of me. "I would like to look at all your shoes. If that would be all right with you?"

I swallowed thickly. "I don't understand. Crystal was my best friend. Why are you interrogating me?"

"I'm not interrogating you. I came here simply to ask you a few questions. You were the last person we know of who saw Crystal alive." He paused to scratch his head. "Yet I must confess many of your answers puzzle me. All last night, you seem to have had no sense of what time it was."

"I told you, I wasn't wearing a watch."

"I understand. But your overall behavior puzzles me. Is it your practice to stay out half the night? In the middle of a school week?"

"I sometimes stay up late. It's not that odd for me."

"Was your mother awake when you came home?"

"No."

"She wasn't worried about where you were?"

"I had called earlier, to say I'd be home soon."

"What time was that?"

"I don't know. It was before I went to the Denny's."

The words were no sooner past my lips than I realized I'd made a mistake. Lt. Lott pounced.

"Wait a second," he said. "You called before you went to the Denny's? But hadn't you just returned from your walk and picked up your car? Why didn't you just step inside and tell your mother where you were going?"

I spoke carefully. "I didn't say I called *just* before I went to the Denny's. I called while I was out on my walk."

"Where did you call from?"

"I can't remember."

"Would you like to wager a guess?"

"I can't remember."

"Can I look at all your shoes?"

"I said you could." I added, "I'll bring them by the station later."

"I can take them with me. If that would be all right with you?"

I acted put out. "Don't you need a search warrant or something to come into my home and take my stuff away?"

"Not if you volunteer the materials willingly."

"I told you, I'll give you the stuff later."

"Would it be all right if, on our way out, we checked what kind of tires you have on your car?"

Damn! My tires would match the tracks beside the road. I hadn't thought of that.

"You've probably already checked them," I grumbled.

"Is that a yes or a no?" Lt. Lott asked.

I shrugged. "I don't care what you do."

"I did warn you before I questioned you that you could have a lawyer present."

I got mad. "Yeah. Sure. My best friend is killed and *I* need a lawyer. I don't understand your priorities, Lieutenant. Why aren't you out trying to catch the murderer?"

Lt. Lott spread his hands. "I don't enjoy these questions any more than you do, Jenny. But it's my job. And you have to admit that you're making my job difficult. You seem to be an intelligent young woman. Think about it carefully and you'll see my dilemma. You dropped Crystal off at twelve. But it might have been eleven, it might have been one. Then, her body is found in the woods, and it seems that she was killed some time between twelve and three in the morning. You see the problem?"

"Explain it to me," I said.

"It's obvious. What you're saying, in essence, is that Crystal was abducted between your dropping her off and before she could reach her front door." He paused. "That seems unlikely, doesn't it?"

"It depends," I said.

"On what?"

"On whether she headed straight for her front door."

Lt. Lott nodded. "I don't mind exploring alternative explanations. Does Crystal have a good friend who lives on her block? Or around the corner?"

"This is a small town. She has friends all over."

"You haven't answered my question."

"Really?" I waited him out.

"Could Crystal have walked to someone else's house at that time of night? Someone she knew well?"

"Sure."

"Could you give me a list of possibilities?" Lt. Lott asked.

"Have you asked her mother for a list?"

"Yes. But now I'm asking you."

I chewed on my lower lip. "Offhand, at that time of night, I can't think of anyone Crystal would walk to see from her house."

"What's your best guess about what happened last night to Crystal?"

"I think someone was waiting for her when I dropped her off."

"Could it have been Amir?"

I forced a laugh. "Amir isn't a murderer. Beside, we'd just left his house."

"But if he followed you, he could have got there just as Crystal was going inside."

"I don't think so," I said. Why was I protecting Amir? Because I had slept with him? I added, "It could have been a stranger who grabbed her."

Lt. Lott nodded. "That's possible. He could have happened by and seen her and grabbed her. But you agree he would have been in a car?"

"Yeah. Or, maybe, he could have had a car nearby." I worried why Lt. Lott was having me run scenarios by him. I suspected he wanted to see what kind of a storyteller I was. Yet I felt it was safer to play his game than to shake my head and act dumb. It had to seem like I wanted to help find the murderer.

"But we have that small problem," Lt. Lott said. "The only footprints we have in the vicinity of the body belong to women. One set we have identified as Crystal's. The other set, of course, we know little about."

A brilliant idea struck me. "Did this other person seem to know the area?"

"What do you mean?"

"You followed his or her footprints, I assume?"

Lt. Lott was cautious. "Yes."

"Did this person seem to know his way around the woods?"

Lt. Lott hesitated. "The footprints wandered throughout the trees."

"Then they were probably the prints of someone lost in the woods. They were probably from someone out of town." I shrugged. "All of us who grew up around here—we all know the woods inside and out."

"Possibly," Lt. Lott said, still holding my eye. "But anyone can get lost in the woods at night. Especially if he or she is upset." He added casually, "I notice those cuts on your right hand. When did you get those?"

My heart almost stopped. "A couple of days ago."

"How did you cut yourself?"

"On a broken glass."

"At home or at work?"

"At home. Here."

"Do you still have the broken glass?"

"I threw it away."

"Trash day is tomorrow. Do you still have the trash bag you put it in?"

"I don't know. I'll look later."

"Would you like to look right now?"

"Not really."

"Why not?"

"Really, Lieutenant Lott. First you want to search through my closet for my shoes. Now you want to go through my garbage. Why don't you just come out and say it—you think I murdered my best friend."

He didn't flinch. "I think you *might* have murdered your best friend."

I snorted. "Get the hell out of my house! Now!"

Lt. Lott stood, along with the talkative cop. The detective did not look angry, only sad. Once more, he spread his hands helplessly.

"I didn't come here suspecting you," he said. "But there are so many holes in your story, I don't know what it will take to dam them up."

I stood. "Why don't you talk to Officer Jakes on your way back to the station. Ask him how close Crystal and I were." There were tears in my eyes. They weren't faked. I couldn't stop thinking about how there were only two sets of prints in the area and what that implied. My voice cracked as I continued, "Then you think about the way you treated me this afternoon. You say it's hard to lose a best friend, but you have no idea how hard it is." My head fell and I wiped at my eyes. "I have nothing to hide."

My outburst did not impress him. "We'll be back later today." He turned toward the door. "Try to be here. If you're not, we'll have to go looking for you. I warn you, Jenny, you don't want that."

CHAPTER 6

GATOR CAME OUT OF HIS ROOM THE MOMENT THE COPS left. I realized he heard everything we'd said. His face was streaked with tears.

"Is Crystal really dead?" he asked.

I hugged him. "Yes. She's dead. Someone killed her in the woods."

"Why did they kill her?"

"I don't know. They were bad people. Bad people do bad things."

He sniffed. "Why were the police mean to you?"

I sighed. "I don't know, Gator."

He pulled back slightly, but continued to hold on to me. "But they were saying you did it. I can tell them you didn't. I can tell them how much you liked Crystal."

I forced a smile. "Thank you. Maybe you should talk to them. But they're police. To them, everyone is suspicious."

"What does *suspicious* mean?"

"It's when someone looks like he did something bad. They think I might have killed Crystal because I was the last one with her that they know about. But I didn't kill her."

"I know that, Jen."

I hugged him again. "What are we going to do?"

"You have to remember better."

I pulled back. "What do you mean?"

"You're having trouble remembering things."

"You noticed that?"

"Yes. I was listening when you talked to the police." He added, "But I won't tell anybody. When Clyde the robot had trouble remembering, he stuck his head in a nuclear reactor." He added, "Could that help you?"

I laughed, although I felt like crying. "I'm afraid that won't work for me. But you're right—I am having trouble remembering things. It's important you keep that secret. It will just make the police more sure that I killed Crystal."

"I promise, I won't tell anyone."

I let go of Gator. "Good. Now I'm going to go

to my room for a while. Don't disturb me. There are some things I have to take care of."

There *was* blood on my sneakers, mixed in with the mud. Washing it off in the bathtub, I wondered if the cops were capable of tearing my pipes apart, finding the traces of blood that way. It seemed I had read about their doing that once before, somewhere. I let the water run a long time.

Once more I checked my sweats. There were no visible bloodstains, but I didn't trust my eyes. Throwing them in the washing machine, I poured in a generous dose of bleach. It would ruin the gray color but I didn't give a damn. Gator peered out at me but quickly withdrew his head when I frowned at him.

I wondered how long it would be before my mother heard the news. I didn't want the police talking to her until I spoke to her. But that Lt. Lott—he was sly. By the time he returned, I knew, he would have found another dozen holes in my story.

With the sweats in the washing machine, I returned to my room. I had delayed too long in examining my personal items. I could not defend myself until I knew who I was.

My bookshelf was a hodgepodge. I was disappointed to see how many cheap romances I'd purchased. Yet there were many classics as well, and a number of fantasy novels. I wasn't a complete flake.

My musical choices were varied. I had punk, grunge, pop, and a ton of sixties CDs. My favorite band seemed to be U2. There was a picture of the lead singer, Bono, on my desk. It was personally signed. Wow. Maybe Crystal got it for me.

I found my diary under my bed, next to a packet of condoms.

Did the adventures with the latter fill the former?

Sitting cross-legged on my bed, I sat down to read my innermost thoughts.

I started reading an entry from six months earlier. Prom night.

May 26th

Oh man, I'm so tired. So drunk, I think if I puke I'll fall facedown in my own vomit. Suffice it to say we had a hell of a night. I better write something about it now 'cause I'm sure I won't remember a thing in the morning.

First off Mitch picked me up late and I chewed him out. Great start, huh? But he looked so cool in his cowboy tux—I couldn't stay mad at him long. Plus he bought me this huge corsage. It was like trying to wear a rose bush. But it was neat, there were no thorns.

Crystal and Harold met us in the lobby of the hotel. Crystal looked totally rad, with her fluffy yellow dress and her hair done up high like the Queen of Persia. But Harold looked like he had just been cut out of a box of cereal. That guy has absolutely no class. I mean, he's nice and all, but I don't know what she sees in him. I would just as soon date a freshman.

The banquet hall was exquisite. There was a crystal chandelier, a live band, candles, food—I felt like dancing all night. Someone spiked the punch, of course, and things got rowdy fast. Halfway through the night, Mitch collapsed in the middle of the dance floor. Or maybe that was me. I have a few fresh bruises I can't explain.

I was happy Crystal was voted prom queen. I don't think I'll ever forget how beautiful she looked, standing up on the platform.

Mitch had reserved a room at the hotel. We tried to do it twice, but the first time Mr. Happy was acting like he needed Prozac, and the second time I rolled off the bed and couldn't get off the floor. It was just as well, we didn't have any condoms with us.

Oh well, I have to go to bed now.

I know my head's going to hurt in the morning.

I paused. Who was this person? Not me, certainly. I wasn't even sure if I liked her. She was funny, granted, but she was also superficial. Harold sounded like a perfectly nice young man to me. Maybe she—I—was so snotty because I was drunk. That was a nice line about how Jennifer had enjoyed Crystal's being voted prom queen.

Flipping forward to the beginning of this school year, I read more.

Sept. 25th

I don't know what's wrong with me. I don't know why I put myself in situations that I don't like and then stay in them.

Mitch is a pain. Mitch is a problem. Mitch is a little boy with a thunderbolt for a right arm and a coconut for a brain. He bets on our own school's teams, but he doesn't always play us to win. What does that do to his performance? I've seen him throw more perfect spirals with a Big Mac and a bag of french fries. Our team lost last night but Mitch was smiling. He says he won two hundred dollars. Like I'm impressed. Those guys he's dealing with are small-time hoods, and he thinks they're big time. Like he's connected now with the Godfather. Those guys don't even look like the mob, they just look mean.

Why don't I leave him? I think it's because of who he's supposed to be. I sure don't stay with him because of who he is. So I guess that makes me a jerk. I sleep with a guy I don't respect and then try to respect myself afterward. It doesn't compute. But I suppose a part of me still loves him, or likes him, or needs him. I'm not sure what the difference is between each of those words. I think it's all a matter of degree.

Crystal met this new guy last night at the Piazza Club. His name's Amir and Crystal says he's so good-looking she forgot to order anchovies on her pizza. What she meant is, she is totally struck by him. Her eyes glow when she says his name. I have to check him out. My eyes haven't glowed in a long time.

Again I paused. This entry interested me more. First, because all my brain cells were working. Second, because I saw where I had already made one mistake with Lt. Lott. Crystal had only known Amir two months. Such a short time to fall in love with a girl and then cheat on her with her best friend.

Then there was my relationship with Mitch. Obviously it was dysfunctional. The guy had a serious gambling problem, and if this morning was any example, he hadn't improved since the beginning of the school year. As an amnesiac I had not trusted him, nor, it seemed, as a long-time girlfriend. My loss of memory had done me one favor. If my memory never came back, I would be able to drop Mitch without feeling any pain.

Mitch's relationship with the local mob made me wonder, though. Those guys were murderers for hire, and they knew how to make it look like somebody else did it. How had Mitch felt about Crystal? Lt. Lott might have been onto something with his questions.

I flipped through the diary, searching for I'm not sure what.

Oct. 15th

Crystal is acting awfully peculiar about Amir. They've been dating three weeks, seeing each other every night, and I have yet to meet the guy! I keep telling her, I won't steal him away, I don't care if he's homely, I won't report him to immigration—but she won't let me meet him. She says he doesn't want to meet me—not yet. I don't buy that. Why wouldn't he want to meet me? He doesn't even know me.

But man, is she hot for this guy. I have never seen Crystal act this way. In chemistry class, she spends most of her time just staring off into space, a stupid smile on her face. True love! It is truly foolish!

I have to admit I'm feeling a tiny bit jealous of Amir. I never realized just how much time I spent with Crystal, how much time we talked on the phone. Now that she's with him every free minute I feel an emptiness. I know it's silly but it's there nevertheless. It is like Crystal is a part of me, and now I am walking around without my left half, or my right side. Oh, well, she'll probably tire of him soon enough.

Mitch is happy Crystal has found a lover. At last, he says, she's out of our hair. But what he doesn't realize is that I am thinking of clipping his locks. And soon.

Gator knocked on the door. I looked up from my diary.

"Yes?"

He poked his head in. "Timmy wants me to come over to his house. Can I go?"

I set the book down. "Sure. Do you want me to take you?"

Gator appeared startled, then recovered. "He's just two houses away. I can walk." He added, "You forgot that."

I sighed. "Yes, Gator, I've forgotten lots of things."

He came farther into the room, touched my knee. "You haven't forgotten me, Jen, have you?"

I laughed. "Don't be silly. How could I forget you?"

He looked worried. "But you called me Ken this morning. You never call me Ken."

I hugged him. "I was just teasing you this morning. I always know a Gator when I see one. They have such big teeth!"

He smiled then, showing me all his teeth. "Better to bite you with!"

I acted afraid. "Oh my."

Then he lost his smile. "Are you having trouble remembering because Crystal died?" he asked seriously.

The question was perceptive. Were the two events related? Clearly they must be. But how? Had my personality fled from the shock of witnessing Crystal's murder? Or had it been erased by the trauma of killing her myself? Neither possibility really made sense. I did not *feel* traumatized. I just felt empty.

"It must have something to do with it," I said finally. "But it doesn't mean I killed Crystal. You know how much I loved her."

Gator nodded. "You loved her as much as you love me."

I smiled sadly. "Yes. That's true. And I would never hurt you."

CHAPTER 7

MITCH CAME OVER BEFORE I COULD RETURN TO MY diary. He'd heard about Crystal. The whole town had. He hugged me and comforted me and talked about what a crazy world we lived in. Then he asked if I had the money he owed Duke. I had to take a step back. We were in the living room.

"Do we have to talk about money now?" I asked.

He shook his head sadly. "I know it's a rotten time, Jen. But if I don't give them their dough tonight, I'll be as bad off as Crystal."

The comparison angered me. "I hardly think so."

He crossed his arms over his chest. "I need the money. I can't put it any more bluntly."

"What if I don't give it to you?"

His face darkened. "I don't think you should threaten me."

I snorted. "Really? What are you going to do to me?"

He grumbled. "I don't need this."

"You have a problem. Why do you have to make it my problem?"

"You're my girlfriend. You're supposed to share my problems."

I got up on my toes. "Do you share my problems?"

"Sure."

"What do you do for me?" I had to wonder.

He shrugged. "Everything. I take you to the movies, buy your meals." He added, "I give you the best sex you've ever had."

"It isn't that great," I muttered.

He was offended. "You're always making snide remarks. I get in a jam, need a little help, and you turn on me. So I have to quit gambling. I know that. I'll quit next week. Tonight I've got to give these guys three hundred dollars. Do you or don't you have it?"

The argument was beginning to bore me. "I don't know. I'll have to look."

His face was full of blood. "You don't know? For Christsakes. How can you not know?"

"Stay here and quit swearing. I'll check in my room."

There were many possible hiding places in my bedroom. But I didn't see Jennifer Hobbs as overly secretive. The first place I checked was my desk, and in the bottom drawer on the left I found a small wooden box filled with twelve twenties. Two hundred and forty dollars. I thought Mitch would be pleased, but when I handed it to him he shook his head.

"It's got to be three hundred," he said.

"Don't you have any money of your own?"

"How can I have money? I play football. I don't work."

"Then how do you take me out?"

"I gamble."

"But you're going to stop gambling. Are you going to stop taking me out?"

"Are you about to have your period or what?" he asked.

I was offended. The sexist pig. "No, I'm not about to have my period. I am mad at you, and I have good reason to be mad. You're here hassling me for money when Crystal is dead. I would laugh if it wasn't so tragic." I threw up my arms. "This is making me sick! Wait here a second. I'll check in Gator's room."

"Duke's people don't take nickels and dimes," he called after me.

Gator did not have a piggy bank, but a large plastic alligator. It was stuffed full of change, with more than a few dollars mixed in. To get to them I had to unscrew the alligator's tail. It took me a few minutes to figure out how to do it, yet in the end I was rewarded with at least sixty in cash, much of it in ones so mangled that it took me another four minutes to flatten them into a reasonable stack. I returned to the living room, happy that I would finally be able to give Mitch what he wanted, and get him off my back. But he wasn't around.

"Mitch?" I said.

"In here," he called from my bedroom.

He must have sneaked in my room while I was fighting with the alligator. Peeking through my door, I was shocked to see Mitch stretched out naked on top of my bed. He was a *big* boy.

"Mitch!" I screamed.

I scared him. He jumped. "What?"

"What are you doing?"

"Nothing. I'm just lying here." Then he seemed to realize, vaguely, that he was stark naked. He gestured to his lower half. "I thought we should do it, you know, Jen, and try to comfort each other."

I stood there with my hands on my hips, about as un-in-the-mood as I could be. "Don't be ridiculous. You're not here to comfort me. You're here to take advantage of me." I threw the money at him. Several of the dollars landed on indiscreet portions of his anatomy. "Take my little brother's hard-earned savings, get dressed, and get the hell out of here. It's over between us."

He sat up in a hurry, trying to catch the dollars as they fell. "What do you mean, it's over?"

"You don't understand? You're that braindead? I mean I don't want to see you anymore. You're not my boyfriend. You're not even a casual acquaintance. You're just a pain in the ass." I turned away. But he stopped me with his next remark, bitter as it was.

"It's that Amir, isn't it? You've got the hots for him. And now that Crystal's dead, you can do more than just look and sweat."

I whipped around. "How dare you suggest that I'd do anything to offend Crystal's memory! At least Amir has honor. He cared about Crystal. He will genuinely mourn her, rather than pay lip service like you do. Get out of my bed. Get out of my life. I hope you end up owing Duke a thousand dollars, and his boys end up breaking your neck instead of your thumbs. Then Carlsrue will have one less phony to worry about."

Mitch stood up, still completely naked. He shook his finger at me.

"You'll regret what you just said, Jen. You'll regret it before the sun goes down."

I glanced out the window and snorted. "The sun has already gone down, egghead. Oh, and prom night, last May. You were pathetic, really. You ruined the whole evening for me, and I want you to know most of the school knows it. A little bird told them." I smiled. "They know your tight spirals get kind of wobbly whenever the action gets too hot. If you know what I mean, Mitch."

He got dressed in a hurry. I sat in the kitchen as he stalked through the living room, his fat greedy hands clutching Gator's dollar bills. There were certain advantages to having no memory. I could say what I wanted without the past filling me with remorse. I laughed as he slammed the front door. At least I was having a little fun before I was locked up.

CHAPTER 8

AMIR APPEARED A FEW MINUTES LATER. IT WAS FORTU-
nate he hadn't run into Mitch because Mitch
might have killed him. Amir didn't look fit to
fight. The news had reached him as well. He
practically collapsed in my arms as he came
through the front door.

"She's dead," he kept saying. "She's dead."

I held him and stroked his hair. "I'm sorry. I'm
so sorry."

He pulled back, his face a mess of tears. "How
can she be dead? We were with her last night. She
was alive; she was fine."

I shook my head. "I don't know how it happened."

He was having trouble breathing. "You know

how I found out? The police showed up at my door and started questioning me about where I was last night. 'Yeah, your girlfriend's dead. Did you do it?' Can you believe they could be that crass?"

I nodded. "They were here as well. They think I killed her."

It was Amir's turn to shake his head. "No. They think *I* killed her. The evil terrorist from the Middle East. They grilled me for an hour. Thank God my landlady was there to tell them I was watching TV with her when Crystal was killed."

I frowned. "You were watching TV with your landlady that late at night?"

"Yeah. I often watch TV with her when she gets off work. You know that."

"But—why?"

"Because I don't have a TV."

"Well, we watched TV, listened to music, ate."

"Oh," I said. "What time did you watch TV till?"

"Jenny? What's wrong? Don't tell me *you* don't believe me."

"No. It's not that. I'm just—curious."

"We watched TV till four in the morning."

"Until four in the morning? That late?"

"There were two old sci-fi monster films on. You know how I like that kind of stuff. And Mrs.

O'Bannon was into the films as well. We hardly noticed how late it was."

"What time did Crystal and I leave?"

"You know. It was about eight-thirty, nine."

"Not later? It couldn't have been later?"

"No. Why are you asking me these questions?"

"Because I told the police we were with you until about twelve."

"Why?"

"Because I couldn't remember when we left."

"It was nowhere near twelve. Jenny, have you lost your mind?"

"Yes. I have lost it. That's exactly what's happened."

He blinked, appeared startled. Then he turned away and sat on the couch. He wiped at his tears with the back of his hand. "What are we going to do?" he asked.

I continued to stand. "About what? Crystal? I'm sorry but we can't do anything about her."

"Why do the police suspect you? I can understand me. In their minds, my skin is the wrong color. You two grew up together. You were her best friend."

"I was the last one to see her alive. Unlike you, I have no alibi for the time she was killed." I added, "I have other strikes against me."

"The fact that you and I were involved?"

"No. They don't know about that." I froze.

"Wait a second. You didn't tell them that we slept together? You wouldn't have told them that."

Amir lowered his head. "I didn't know what to tell them. They had obviously questioned you. They wouldn't tell me what you said. I knew if they caught me in a lie, I'd be in for it. I could be deported."

I took a step toward him, glared down. "You didn't tell them that you and I had sex?"

His face was consumed with anguish. "I had to!"

"Why?"

"Because I figured you had."

"That's ridiculous! I wouldn't blab to anybody that I was screwing my best friend's boyfriend." I turned away, furious. "Now they have a motive. They can prop me up in court and say she murdered her best friend for the oldest reason in the book. She wanted his man."

"I'll tell them it's not true."

I whirled on him. "You'll tell them! You're the one who just got me hung."

"They won't hang you. Don't worry, they don't do that."

"Oh, yeah? Does Oregon have the death penalty?"

He considered. "Yeah." He added, "But they use lethal injection. Not hanging."

"Oh, that's a relief. I feel a whole lot better

now. I don't have to worry about my pretty neck. They're going to shoot poison in my veins. You have a lot of nerve telling me not to worry."

Amir was perplexed. "They won't find you guilty of murder. You didn't murder her." He paused. "You didn't, did you?"

I was exasperated. "No. I don't murder people! It's not something I do."

"Then what are you worried about? And why are you shouting at me?"

"Because you're so stupid! You're more stupid than Mitch. And he has a rock for a brain. You handed Lieutenant Lott the one piece of information he needs to arrest me. A motive. Now the fact that I was Crystal's best friend is meaningless. In fact, it works against me."

"But you didn't kill her." He paused. "Where did you go after you dropped Crystal off?"

"Out."

"Where?"

"I just went out." I added, "I went to Denny's for something to eat."

"What time did you go to Denny's?"

I lowered my voice. "Around two. And don't go telling the police that."

Amir was shocked. "What did you do between nine and two?"

"I went for a walk."

"You walked for five hours? That's hard to believe."

Feeling weary, I plopped down on the couch beside him. "You're telling me," I muttered.

"I don't understand. What are you saying?"

I spoke to the floor. "I can't remember what I did last night."

"After you left my house?"

My lower lip trembled. "Yes. After I left your house. I simply can't remember what I did."

Amir's voice was gentle. "But you said you went to Denny's. You remember that much." He added, "Don't you?"

I leaned back in the couch and nodded. "Yeah. I remember that much. But I don't know what I was doing when Crystal was killed."

"Do you at least remember where you were?"

I hesitated. "I was nowhere."

"Maybe you just came home and went to sleep for a few hours."

"Maybe."

"Why don't you ask your mother?"

"I can't."

"Why not?"

"Because she knows I didn't come home."

Amir was silent for a long while. "Are you sure you want to talk to me about these things?" he asked finally. "It might be better if you didn't."

I forced a chuckle. "And who am I supposed to talk to about these things?"

"Maybe a lawyer."

I gave him a dirty look. "I didn't kill her. I knew her a hell of a lot longer than you did. And I loved her more than you did."

Amir stared at me. "Did you?" he asked quietly.

I met his stare. "Yes, I did. Remember, you only showed up a couple of months ago." I added, bitter, "You weren't that big a part of our lives."

"I liked to think I was."

"You cheated on her."

He sighed. "We both did. And now she's dead, and we can't say we're sorry."

"It's better she died not knowing." I added, "But of course everybody else is going to know now. Her mother, her father. Have you spoken to them?"

"Yes. They don't understand why you haven't called."

"I will. How did they sound?"

"How do you think? Terrible. Crystal's father —they had to sedate him."

"Have the police told them that I'm their prime suspect?"

"No. And don't say that. It's not true."

"Hang around until Lieutenant Lott returns.

You'll see how true it is." I added, "I think I should pack an overnight bag. I might be sleeping behind bars tonight. But what should I take with me? A file? A box of dynamite? Mustn't make hasty decisions. The stuff might have to last me forty years."

He stood. "You're babbling. The police know how to make everyone feel guilty. This will all get straightened out. The main thing is—we have to mourn Crystal, and then we have to heal. That's going to take time. But we can do this better as friends than as enemies." He paused. "I'm sorry for what I told the police, Jenny. I honestly didn't say it to harm you. I still want to be your friend."

I looked up at him. "Do you still want to screw me?"

He took a step back. "This is hardly the time."

I gave him a twisted smile. "I wasn't offering you my body. I was just wondering—that's all. With Crystal dead, do you still have the guts or the heart or the whatever you want to call it to be involved with me? Treat it as a hypothetical question. I'm not necessarily saying I want to be with you."

He looked out the window at the other houses, the distant trees. Incredibly, from my front window, I could see the beginning of the woods where I had awakened beside the pond. I wondered if Amir knew where Crystal had died.

"Yes," he said finally.

"You want to screw me?"

"No. I want to be your friend." He turned toward the door. "I'll call you later to see how you're doing. Try to relax."

I knew then I was the most powerful creature in the world.

I didn't know why my dream came back to me right then. Obviously it had a Middle Eastern flavor, with the hashish smoking and all. And the black veil over the witchy woman would remind anyone of women in a Moslem society. Yet there was nothing specific that connected my dream to Amir. He had not been in any of the scenes. There had been only me and the witch. And the Tarot cards and the knife and the witch's blood. But why had I been smoking such a potent drug? Why had I been gazing up at the stars and thinking I could touch them?

"Amir?" I said.

He was at the door. "Yes?"

"When did you come to this country?"

"You know. Two months ago."

"You speak such fluent English."

"Thank you."

"What country are you from?"

"You know. Egypt."

"Did you live near the Nile?"

"Yes."

"Is it lovely at night?"

"Yes. Very lovely. Look, I'll try to call you later—"

"Amir," I interrupted, staring at the far wall, trying hard to remember, trying hard to exist, as a person.

"Yes?"

"Did you ever smoke hashish?"

"No."

"But it's common in that part of the world, isn't it?"

"Yes. It's very common."

"Did you know anyone who did smoke hash?"

"Sure. Lots of people."

"What did it do to them?"

He hesitated. "Many things."

"Bad things?"

"It's a powerful drug. What can I say?"

I finally looked over at him. My questions seemed to disturb him, but only slightly. "Do you have any brothers? Or sisters?"

He took a breath. "I had two sisters."

"They're dead?"

"Yes."

"I'm sorry. Were you close to them?"

"Yes." He paused. "There were three of us. We were triplets."

I nodded. Somehow, that sounded right, like I knew it because I remembered it. But I also knew he had never told me before. Certainly he acted like he hadn't. A set of triplets. Amazing.

"How did they die?" I asked.

"Jenny."

"I'm sorry, but I really want to know. I think I need to know."

He lowered his head. "They were murdered."

"Was the murderer ever caught?"

He was a long time answering. "No. He got away."

I nodded. "Crystal's murderer won't get away. I'm sure of it."

He stared at me a long time before he left.

CHAPTER 9

My head hurt. My heart ached. I couldn't take any more. Going into my bedroom, I closed the door and lay down. I was out before I knew it.

Once more, I dreamed.

Egyptian pyramids shimmered in the far distance, beneath the white light from the moon, the stars—how glorious the nighttime sky was. It wasn't unusual for my senses to be acute when my blood was boiling. If the eyes were the windows of the soul then drugs were glass cutters. My windows had not been simply opened, but cut out. The hashish percolated in my brain like steam from a witch's brew. I had a witch with me as we hiked up into the hills far out in the country. She had brought me to this place, not the other way around. Before I embarked on my insane odyssey, she said, she needed to show me something.

On the summit of the hill we were climbing was a graveyard. Yet there stood no tombstones or plaques, only ancient statues of demons entangled in bitter fighting, warring gods wielding sharp swordlike weapons, and large stone disks on which were written the library of a language four thousand years forgotten. Still, it was a place of the dead. I smelled it as I looked around in wonder.

"I have never heard an archaeologist mention this spot," I said.

The witch stood near me. I wasn't sure she wouldn't take a knife to me if she had the chance. Yet there was a longing in her eyes as she looked at me, fear even—but for me, not of me. Her black veil had been left behind. Stepping around the various stone statues, she gestured to the entire hilltop.

"We stand on private land," she said. "Few know about this place."

I spoke sarcastically. "Why are you one of the chosen few?"

Her mood was forgiving somehow. She wasn't offended. "Because this land belongs to my family, your family. The things we have found over the last centuries have been kept hidden here." She pointed to the statue of the three entangled demons and added, "The world is not ready for what this place has to say." Then she pointed to me. "You are not ready either. But you have to be told. You demand to be told."

I shook my head, not understanding her. "I just want the girl," I said. "What does this place have to do with her?"

She moved closer to me and sat at my feet on a stone pedestal. Looking up at me, her eyes glittered in the moonlight and I was reminded not so much of a witch but of an ancient deity. Of course, there were spirits of light and darkness and I was not sure what part she played tonight. Nor did I care. I just wanted the girl who had begun to haunt my dreams, my waking moments even—a vision of light glimpsed through heavy shadows. The girl I saw when I looked in the mirror, but whose face was not my own. The American. I knew that much about her.

"Sit beside me," she said, patting the stone. "There is much you need to hear."

I remained stubborn. "I prefer to stand."

Her tone sharpened. "For what I am about to tell you, you should kneel. But that is not your nature, is it? Your arrogance is matched only by your indulgences."

I touched my head. "I take drugs to push aside the veil. Not for pleasure."

"Then why do you feel you must find this girl? Isn't that for pleasure?"

I shook my head. "You wouldn't understand."

"But I do understand. What you experience, the visions of others, I had them, too, when I was your age."

I became interested. She had never spoken that way to me before. "I do not see others," I said. "I see only one. The girl."

"But there is another besides her. There always is. He or she may even be nearby."

"What are you saying?"

"That your use of drugs has pushed the veil aside too far, and torn it in places. Your enlightenment is false. You try to peer into the secret mysteries without first taking the beginning steps."

I *was* haughty. I knew the power of my enlightenment. I had seen the soul, and now there was nothing in the world I could not have. Yet even I did not understand why I wanted the girl so much. That was the main reason I continued to listen to this woman whom I had scorned since I was a child.

"What are these beginning steps?" I asked.

"The virtues. Before you can become a god

you must become a perfect person. You must have honesty, compassion, generosity, and patience. Then the true teacher will appear, then the mysteries will be revealed. But now you want it all. Your drug-induced trances are shams. True, you see glimpses of the truth, but that truth just serves to torment you."

I laughed. "You should talk. You're every bit the sinner I am. I notice you didn't list chastity as a virtue. Was that because you spent half your life as a harlot?"

The reflected moonlight in her eyes turned cold. "You can mock me if you must. But you still need me. You cannot find the girl without me. And you do not know what will happen if you do find her, and bring her together with the other—in your presence. You think you have seen the soul, but I tell you that you have seen only its illusion."

"What is that?" I asked, interested. The old woman did seem to know a thing or two. Yet she shook her head in response to my question. Then she sat silently with her eyes closed, as if listening to voices only she could hear. A shudder seemed to go through her and her eyes popped open. Her gaze strayed to the statue of the three warring demons, then to me. She blinked as if recognizing the similarities between us. Again she shook her head. I didn't understand why a tear had sprung from her right eye. She did not care for me any more than I cared for her. So I thought.

"I've changed my mind," she said. "I brought you to this ancient place to warn you, but you will not listen. I see that now. I should have seen it earlier. You would just use the knowledge I would give you to destroy others. It is your nature." She stood to leave. "This is the last time we will meet. I don't care what you say or do. You will have to follow this path you have chosen alone. But I can tell you where it will lead—to madness and death."

I grabbed her arm as she stepped by. "Don't go," I said softly. "Please? Tell me this great secret."

She stared at me. "Let me go."

I tightened my grip. "I really want to know," I said.

"You don't deserve to know."

With my free hand, I slowly took my knife from my robe. "Then you don't deserve to live."

Her eyes went wide, but she continued to stare at me. "You would not kill your own mother," she whispered.

I held the knife to her throat and laughed. "I would take great pleasure in killing you." I brushed the blade lightly across her flesh. A dark trickle of blood crept down her neck. She went still, but nevertheless swallowed, and that slight movement brought even more blood. The sight of it did strange things to my mind. Things even the drugs had been unable to do. The statue of entwined demons seemed to stir beside us. I leaned over and spoke softly in her ear. "Tell me. . . ."

CHAPTER 10

WHEN I AWOKE, MY MOTHER WAS SITTING BESIDE ME on the bed. She had interrupted my dream. Without her coming, I would have heard what the old woman had to say. Not knowing was frustrating. The dreams were the only link I had to my past life. I was sure they had something to do with the fact that I had lost my memory.

My mother had been crying and looked little like the bright professional woman who had said goodbye to me that morning. Her makeup was smeared, her eyes were red. Her right hand, as she reached over to brush the hair from my face, shook. She had heard the news as well.

But maybe not all of it.

"The police came to the clinic," she whispered. "They told me about Crystal. Then they started asking all these questions about you."

I took my mother's hand and sat up. "What did you tell them?"

"I told them to get out of my clinic."

I hugged her. "Good for you."

But my mother drew back. "They think you killed Crystal."

I nodded, grim. "Yeah, I'm their number-one suspect. Isn't that crazy?"

"But why do they suspect you? Everyone in town knows you two were the best friends there could be."

"Lieutenant Lott doesn't believe much in friendship." I paused. "He was the cop who told me Crystal was dead. I practically went into shock, and then he started asking me all these questions, and jumping on me every time I said something that didn't match my previous answers. He had my head spinning."

"He's the one who came by the clinic," my mother said.

"I think he'll be back later." I glanced at the clock. It was seven-twenty.

"But I still don't understand," my mother said. "What did you say, specifically, that made him suspect you?"

"I got messed up on the times. When I saw Crystal, when I dropped her off."

"When did you drop her off at home?"

"I don't remember exactly. Ten o'clock."

"But you saw her after that? You told me you spoke to her."

I sighed. "I just told you that to put your mind at rest. Actually, after I left her at her house, I didn't see her."

"Where were you all last night?"

"Mother! I didn't kill her!"

She hugged me quickly. "Of course you didn't, Jen. I know that. And I know how painful this must be for you. But you've got to get your story straight. Especially if that detective is coming back tonight." She paused. "Do you want me to call an attorney?"

I swung my legs off the side of the bed. "I don't need an attorney," I said flatly.

"But you might want to talk to one just the same. Find out what your rights are. I mean, I don't even know if we have to let Lieutenant Lott in our house."

I stood. "I'm going out."

"Where are you going?"

"To Crystal's house. I haven't spoken to her mother yet."

"Maybe you should call her first."

I reached for my shoes, the same pair I had on

when I woke up beside the pond. "I don't need to call. I've been going over there since I was a kid."

"What if the detective comes?"

"Tell him I'm out murdering another good friend."

"Jenny!"

"Tell him that I've gone out for a walk. That I often walk at night." I squeezed my mother's shoulder as I turned to leave. "He'll love to hear that."

My mother grabbed my arm. Her eyes, as she looked at me, were so sad. Crystal must have been like a second daughter to her.

"Why would anyone want to kill her?" she asked.

"I don't know." I remembered a line from my dream. "Maybe it just had to end this way. In madness and death."

I took my phone book with me as I left, which fortunately contained Crystal's address. My map was a big help. After studying it, I decided to drive to the Denger residence rather than walk. Their house was about a mile away. I knew Lt. Lott would freak out if he drove up and my car was gone but I didn't care.

I remembered my book had Amir's address as well.

I'd visit him next.

I was tired of people coming to see me. Of my sitting around not knowing what was happening. I was going on the offensive.

Yet I had picked a bad place to start. Just walking up to the Denger residence, I could feel the grief. It hung over the house like gas from a swampy graveyard. When Crystal's mother answered the door, she stared at me for several seconds without recognition. I couldn't hold it against her, of course, since she was a total stranger to me. But then she nodded weakly and reached to open the door.

"Jenny," she said. "Please come in."

The interior of the house was dark. A single lamp in the corner of the living room was the only illumination for both the living room and kitchen. It was as if the Dengers' pain would become more real if the two of them could see each other clearly. Yet Mr. Denger was nowhere to be seen. Then I remembered Amir's comment about his being sedated. From the pictures on the walls, it didn't appear as if Crystal had any brothers or sisters. Mrs. Denger gestured for me to take a seat. She did likewise, settling in a chair across from me.

What do you say to a mother who has just lost her only child? Mrs. Denger's face looked as if a psychic weight had been dropped on it from out of a black astral plane. Her eyes continued to blink; she couldn't stop clasping and unclasping her fingers. I felt like an intruder with ulterior motives. And in a sense, that was true. I needed to get into Crystal's bedroom, understand better who she was so I could understand better why she had died.

"I'm sorry I didn't call before coming," I began. "I just needed to see you, to tell you how sorry I am."

The woman nodded. "It's good to see you, Jenny. It's always good."

"How's Mr. Denger?"

"Awful. The doctor gave him a shot." She glanced down the hall. "He might be waking up soon."

The way she said the last words, it was as if it were an awful prospect. "If he's not up before I leave," I said, "tell him I was asking about him."

"I will."

I sniffed. "I feel so terrible about all this. I don't know what to say."

"There's nothing you can say, Jenny."

"The police. They think I had something to do—"

"Forget them," Mrs. Denger interrupted, waving her hand. "I told them that I would be as much a murder suspect as you. I don't know what's wrong with that detective."

"I made myself a suspect by giving several

113

confused answers to his questions." I added, "He quizzed me right after informing me of Crystal's death. I think I was in shock."

Mrs. Denger nodded. "I told him the same thing. But he remained skeptical." She buried her face in her hands. "How are they going to find this murderer if they waste their time chasing people like you?"

"I don't know."

Mrs. Denger looked up. "But the detective said you brought Crystal home. You didn't, did you?"

I shifted uncomfortably. "I did. I dropped her out front."

"What time was that?"

"Around ten."

"I was still awake then. I didn't hear your car."

"I just swung by and she jumped out." I added, "That was the last I saw of her."

Mrs. Denger shivered. "Then the murderer must have grabbed her outside our own door. How could such a thing happen in Carlsrue? We've never had any violence here."

"It makes no sense."

"You didn't see anyone, did you?"

"No."

Mrs. Denger stared off into the distance. A faint smile touched her lips. "Was she happy, her last night out?"

"Yes. We had a good time. We were with Amir."

"She loved Amir a great deal."

"Yes. He was over at my house today. He was very upset."

"The poor boy. He was Crystal's first real love, you know. She never really cared for Harold. I mean, she liked him but . . . Amir was special to her." She paused. "Are the police bothering him as well?"

"Not really. He was at home with his landlady when Crystal—when it happened. He was watching TV with the woman."

"I see."

"Mrs. Denger. May I ask a favor?"

"Yes. Anything."

"May I sit in Crystal's bedroom for a little while? I always liked her room. We had so many long talks in there. I think just being there will, you know, help me feel like she's not really gone." I had to dab at my eyes—I wasn't faking. "Everything inside feels so empty."

Mrs. Denger was sympathetic. "Why, of course you can. And in the future, you come over any time you wish."

The moment I entered the room, I turned on the light and discreetly closed the door. I would have locked it had there been a lock.

The room was much neater than mine. Had Mrs. Denger cleaned it up? Or had Crystal a premonition of her death and decided to tidy up before she left the planet? Or did everyone who woke up the morning they were to die have such a vision? The questions disturbed me.

Because, all of a sudden, I believed I wouldn't live to see tomorrow's sun.

"Oh God," I whispered, sitting down on a corner of her bed. Where had that certainty come from? Was there something in the room that inspired it? Looking around, I saw a possibility. A small leather-bound red book sitting on top of Crystal's desk. It was identical to mine. We had probably bought them at the same store. Or else she had bought two, and given me one as a gift. From what I had heard of Crystal, she was a giving person.

It was Crystal's diary.

It was as if it had been set out for me to find.

But by whom? Her?

The other?

Sitting down at her desk, I opened the book to one of the last entries. They were the only ones that mattered. The ones where the Grim Reaper had stood behind her as she wrote. Her last will and testament. I shivered as I scanned the words, written in a firm script with what looked like a Flair pen. The window was slightly open; the room was cold. But the chill that settled into my bones as I read had nothing to do with room temperature. Carlsrue was the setting for a soap opera, and I had yet to realize how many roles one character could play.

Oct. 29th

I can't contain myself anymore. I must tell Jenny the truth about Mitch, but I'm afraid to break her heart. Yet I have to wonder if she loves Mitch as much as she pretends to. Maybe she'll welcome what I have to say. Still, I hesitate. I have never enjoyed bringing people bad news.

Mitch is cheating on Jenny. Last night I saw him in Baker with Kathy Kahn, parked outside the theater. The movie hadn't started —the doors weren't even open—yet the previews were already rolling. The way they were making out, there was no way he was going home dissatisfied. Kathy's a tramp— she knows Mitch is dating Jenny. But Mitch is a thousand times worse. How could he do such a thing to her, after all she's done for him?

I couldn't stand it. I couldn't walk away. I strode up to his car and pounded on the window. When he saw me, his face went white. Kathy just looked up and grinned. I stood there and demanded that Mitch roll down the window. He took his sweet time.

"What's going on?" I asked when we were face to face.

"Crystal. Hi. What are you doing here?"

"I came to see the movie. It's not playing in Carlsrue. You should have thought of that, you know. People from Carlsrue often come here. I don't know what bothers me more— that you're doing this behind Jenny's back or that you're so sloppy about it. I can't be the only one who's seen you parked here tonight."

Mitch was at a loss for words. "Well," he said. "It's not exactly the way it looks."

"Really? How is it not the way it looks?"

"Well, you see, you don't know this about Jenny, but she's not always straight with you in this department. If you get my meaning."

"Jenny's straight as they come. I don't get your meaning."

He glanced at Kathy and then smirked, which made me want to sock him. "Then there's no explaining it to you," he said.

He was implying that Jenny was cheating on him, that it was sporting season all round. But he was lying through his teeth. Jenny would never two-time anyone.

I don't know how I can tell her.
And I don't know how I cannot tell her.

The entry did nothing to lesson my guilt. Hastily, I flipped to another page, closer to today's date.

Nov. 12th

Amir and I made love last night. It wasn't the first time, of course, but it was the hardest time. Yet I don't mean the sex. That was wonderful, as always. It was lying in his arms afterward, at his place.

It was late and I began to doze. If he hadn't shifted in bed, I might have slept through the entire night, which my mother would have loved. But as it was, he disturbed me just as I slipped into a dream. As I came fully awake, I realized I'd had this same dream before. Several times.

It takes place in Egypt, beside the Nile. That should not seem so strange since I'm dating a guy from that part of the world. But in this dream I don't act like I would normally act. I mean, I've had all kinds of dreams where I've been in sword fights and gun fights and killed people even. I'm sure everyone does. In this dream I have a knife that I am quick to use whenever I am annoyed. But none of these details are that strange. The weird thing is my state of mind. In the dream, I'm in someone else's mind. And I don't even think I'm a female, although I'm not sure. I'm almost always intoxicated, and there is an old woman with a black veil covering half her face who hovers near me. We're related, I think, but I don't like her. In this dream, I always feel like cutting her throat.

I don't know how many times I've had this nightmare, but it definitely is a nightmare. When I woke up I was relieved to be out of it. But I think it started shortly after I met Amir. Maybe I should ask him about it. He would probably just laugh.

I love him so much!

If he ever left me, I think, I would just shrivel up and die.

"Jenny."

The voice made me jump. I looked up to see Mr. Denger. I assumed it was him. He didn't look well. A tall man with thin graying hair and cheeks sunken in with grief, he resembled a corpse someone had forgotten to embalm. Even his eyes, with the yellowed whites, were sunk in his head. He saw I was reading Crystal's diary and the beginning of a scowl touched his face. But he didn't have the strength to complete the expression. He did not have the energy. Clearly his daughter had been the light of his life. I closed the book.

"I'm sorry," I said hastily. "Crystal's diary was lying out and I just picked it up." I gestured helplessly. "I didn't mean to pry, Mr. Denger."

He forced a faint smile. He forgave me. "Of course you didn't, Jenny. I know you feel this loss as much as we do. I know . . ."

He was unable to complete the sentence. A wave of grief consumed him and he buried his face in his hands against the door. I was on my feet in a moment, patting him on the back, whispering soothing words that did nothing to soothe him. It was too much, really, to lose an only child. There was nothing you could say to either parent that made any sense. She's in heaven now. Her suffering has ended. She's happy. And that worst of all lines—don't worry. Yet, in a sense, that was the most honest line. There was nothing to worry about at this stage of the game. When all hope died, worry was a mere afterthought. I had to steady Mr. Denger to keep him on his feet. He mumbled something about having to go to the morgue, to view his daughter.

I didn't offer to come.

I left the diary, wanting to read more.

Perhaps I could come back for it later.

But not too late, I swore. Before tomorrow's sun rose.

We had been close friends.

But even close friends didn't share the exact same dreams.

CHAPTER 11

AMIR'S PLACE WAS ON THE WRONG SIDE OF THE tracks, literally and figuratively. The trains passed not sixty feet from his room, which was tucked under the eaves above a garage where garbage collected on top of junk. His landlady, the burly sixty-year-old woman who answered the door on the ground level, looked like something grown in a burlap bag in a primitive lab. She had a hump for a back, which forced her head forward, her shoulders down. Her scraggly gray hair was steel wool. Breathing did not come easily for her. Looking me up and down with beady brown eyes, she wheezed in and out of congested lungs. I decided the rent had to be reasonable.

"Hi," I said. "Is Amir here?"

Mrs. O'Bannon—I remembered her name from what Amir had said—gestured to a door at the top of the stairs that went up the side of the garage. "I think I heard him go out a few minutes ago. Did you try knocking?"

Her voice was surprisingly kind, gentle to the ears. I regretted having judged her so quickly on her appearance. I wondered if that was something I used to do. The cockiness of my written words in my diary continued to bother me. Crystal, on the other hand, had sounded much nicer in her diary.

"I'll try in a second." I added as I started to turn, "I guess you heard about what happened to Crystal?"

Mrs. O'Bannon nodded sadly. There was genuine pain on her face. Crystal and she must have become friends over the last couple of months.

"Such a terrible thing," she said. "And she was such a bright girl. I'm going to miss her. I'm sure you and Amir will as well."

"You know it happened last night?"

"I heard. After you two girls left here."

"Yes. I dropped Crystal off and then—that's all I know. Amir doesn't know anything either. He says he was here, watching TV with you."

She coughed weakly and then nodded. "We stayed up late watching two movies. I didn't want to, but Amir insisted. Personally, they bored me to death." She sighed. "If I'd known what was happening at the time, I couldn't have watched them. I kept falling asleep. That's why I'm so tired today."

"There were two old sci-fi monster films on. You know how I like that kind of stuff. And Mrs. O'Bannon was into the films as well. We hardly noticed how late it was."

"I thought you liked sci-fi," I said.

"Who told you that?"

"Amir."

"I don't know why he said that. I told him a dozen times last night I couldn't stand it."

"Why didn't you just kick him out of your house?"

"I tried to. He wouldn't go. He looked kind of sick anyway. I made him a bowl of chicken soup but he didn't eat it." She added, "You know the police were here already, asking what he was doing at the time of Crystal's death. I think they asked just because he's from the Middle East."

"What else did they ask?"

"The usual. How Crystal and Amir got along. I didn't mention any of their fights."

"They fought?"

The woman appeared surprised. "You know that, Jenny. They fought like animals. We've talked about this before."

I nodded. "Yeah, I remember. Hey, would it be OK if I waited in Amir's place until he came back?"

She considered a moment. "I suppose that would be all right. But I'll have to let you in. He never leaves without locking up. Not that he has anything in there worth stealing. He's a month behind on the rent." She laughed softly. "He's lucky he has a landlady like me. An ugly old woman who can't count."

"You're not ugly, Mrs. O'Bannon, and you're not old," I said firmly. "You're perfect the way you are."

My compliment surprised her. "Well, thank you, Jenny. That was kind of you."

"But you still can't count," I added, joking.

She smiled. "The world is filled with too many people who are only interested in counting. I told Amir he could pay when he has it. He's a trustworthy young man."

"Yeah," I agreed out loud. But I had to wonder.

Mrs. O'Bannon let me in and left me alone. It was a *studio* apartment, but that word was much too eloquent for the place. It was so tiny that Amir could bump his arms on the ceiling trying to put on a shirt. He had a foam rubber mat on the floor for a bed, a hot plate for a stove. His solitary closet was the size of a kitchen cabinet. Peeking inside it, I was appalled to see how few clothes he had. Two shirts, two pairs of pants, and a leather coat that didn't look as if it would keep an Oregon winter away. He must have come to our country on a shoestring.

Our country. What belonged to me? Not even my own mind.

Yet the place was tidy, meticulously so. It was as if he cleaned up each time before he left the apartment. I wondered what Amir did for money, if he had a job. Or even a green card that would allow him to stay in the country for extended periods of time. Yet he must have been here before, I thought. His English was not merely fluent, his accent was pure Northwest American. He didn't sound foreign at all.

Feeling only a minor pang of conscience, I began to search through what few possessions he had. I mean, I was supposed to be sleeping with the guy. I could at least see if he kept a knife stashed under his pillow.

I didn't find a knife, but came up with something else of interest, under his foam rubber mat.

A hash pipe. I recognized it immediately.

Did that mean I smoked hashish as well?

Before I took off my clothes for him.

"Did you ever smoke hashish?"

"No."

"What did it do to them?" I said aloud, remembering. "Many things."

Amir had lied to me. I found a small stash of the drug a few minutes later, stuffed in a Tylenol bottle in his medicine cabinet. The drug was dark colored, soft as partially dried clay. The smell was both bitter and sweet. Just sniffing it made my head spin. Yet I knew beyond any doubt that it was hashish. I must have held it before. Yet I couldn't have because then Amir would never have lied to me about using it, or not using it. His lie, the whole situation, was a paradox.

I had held the drug, though. In my blood. In my nightmares.

"What a coincidence," I whispered.

Yet what did any of this mean? That Amir had killed Crystal? He was the one person in the world who absolutely could *not* have killed her. He had a foolproof alibi. Mrs. O'Bannon was not lying. He had been with her the whole night.

He had gone out of his way to be with her the whole night.

After putting the drug and the pipe back, I hurried down the exterior steps. The landlady took her time answering the door. From her drowsy eyes, she looked as if she had just lain down to take a nap. But she smiled when she saw it was me.

"Yes, Jenny? Do you want to watch TV all night as well?"

I forced a smile. "No. I was just wondering about a comment you made. You said Amir was kind of sick last night. What was wrong with him?"

She scratched her head. "It was strange, actually. He was watching the movies with me, like I said, but it wasn't as if he was really watching them. His gaze was distant, fixed. When I spoke to him, he'd only mumble. When I offered him the chicken soup, he scarcely glanced at it. I thought he might be loaded or something." She paused to lower her voice. "He doesn't do drugs, does he?"

I thought for a moment. "I don't know what Amir does."

CHAPTER 12

LT. LOTT WAS WAITING FOR ME WHEN I GOT HOME. HE had come alone. From the expression on my mother's face, it appeared as if he had been there a long time, saying disturbing things about me. I scowled at him as I came through the front door. I wanted to stay on the offensive.

"What do you want now?" I asked bluntly.

He stood. His face was harder than it had been earlier. Obviously he had gathered more facts to support his suspicions. "I told you not to leave the house," he said.

"I didn't know I was in the military and had to follow your orders," I replied, removing my coat and hanging it on a hook just inside the door. I added casually, "Hi, Mom."

My mother was not happy with my attitude. "Maybe you should sit down, Jenny, talk to the lieutenant."

I headed down the hall. "After I use the bathroom."

"Jenny," Lt. Lott called after me.

"Don't worry, I just have to take a pee. I'm not going to kill anybody."

I did not go straight to my bedroom, but entered Gator's. He was sitting on his bed putting together a puzzle of the Big Bad Wolf and Little Red Riding Hood. He looked so relieved to see me, it almost broke my heart. He got up on his knees and gave me a big hug.

"Are they going to put you in jail?" he asked.

"No, of course not. I didn't do anything wrong."

He let go of me and nodded vigorously. "That's what I tried to tell the policeman, but Mom made me go to my room. I wanted to explain how Crystal was your best friend in the whole world. Besides me."

I laughed softly. "You can't be my *best* friend. You're my brother."

He spoke seriously. "I don't know. I was thinking I should be your best friend now that you don't remember having a brother."

"Gator, I told you. I do remember you."

He was doubtful. "I know sometimes when

you get older you forget things. A lady on TV said that."

I messed up his hair. "I'm not that old, and I'm never going to forget you, so relax. But there is something I need you to do for me. Something very secret and dangerous."

He was interested. "What is it?"

I leaned close and spoke softly. "I need you to go to Crystal's house right now. I know how late and dark it is, but you'll be OK if you take your bike. I need her diary. It's sitting on top of her desk in her bedroom. It's a small red book. But you can't go to the front door and ask her parents if you can take it. They might not be there, and if they are, they probably wouldn't let you have it."

"I have to steal it?"

"You're going to borrow it, not steal it."

He was eager, but also confused. "If I can't talk to them, how am I going to get in?"

"Her bedroom window is open. I was just there. You should be able to slide inside without any trouble. You know which bedroom is hers?"

"Sure. *My* memory is OK."

"Good. If you see they're home, you have to be careful to be especially quiet. Grab the diary and come right back here."

"Can I tell Mom I'm going?"

"No. You can't tell anyone. And you have to go right now, while Mom and I are busy with the lieutenant. Go out this window. Don't forget a jacket."

His face glowed with pleasure. "This is like spy stuff."

I smiled. "You are a spy. You're my spy."

But his joy faltered. "If you get the diary, can you prove you didn't kill Crystal?"

I nodded. "That's the idea."

Gator left right away. I had seen his bike was parked around the side of the house. He said he loved to ride it in the dark, but knew to watch out for cars.

Back in the living room, my mother and Lt. Lott were waiting for me. I sat beside my mom on the couch and crossed my legs. The detective seemed to be ready to snap at me but changed his mind as I stared at him. Still, he was not there to tell me a bedtime story.

"Where were you just now?" he asked.

"Talking to my little brother in his bedroom," I said.

"Before that?" he said with a trace of impatience.

"I visited Crystal's family, and then I visited Amir." I added, "But he wasn't home, so I talked to his landlady instead."

"Why did you go to those two places?"

"Is this another interrogation?"

"Yes," he said flatly.

I turned to my mother. "Why haven't you kicked him out?"

My mother was a bundle of nerves. "He has a warrant to examine our house."

"I see." I turned back to the detective. "Am I under arrest?"

"Not yet," he replied.

"Then I don't have to answer your questions," I said.

"That's entirely up to you," he said smoothly. "You can remain silent, or you can ask for an attorney to be present. Still, if you are innocent, I think it would be in your best interests to talk to me now."

"Why?" I asked.

"For a number of reasons. Our people have spent the day at the crime scene. We have several pieces of evidence that place you at the scene of the crime."

I forced a laugh. "Such as?"

"The tire tracks we found by the side of Highway Seventeen—a mile from the pond beside where Crystal was murdered—match the treads on your Celica."

"I have Michelin tires," I said. "Lots of people do."

"But yours are special Michelins. The treads on yours match the tracks at the highway." He paused. "Are you sure you and Crystal weren't walking in the woods late last night?"

"I'm sure."

"Near where we found Crystal's body, we also found a number of long brunette hairs. It was as if the woman in question had been lying on the ground not more than twenty feet from Crystal, for a period of several hours." He paused. "Those hairs, in color and length, would seem to match yours. I suspect when we do a DNA analysis, we will discover that it is, in fact, your hair."

I swallowed thickly. I kept forgetting the tools police had these days. DNA and electron microscopes and orbital satellites—they'd be able to build a foolproof case against me no matter how tough I acted.

"Did you find any evidence that a third party was also present?" I asked carefully.

"No," he said flatly. "None."

That took me a moment to absorb. But there had to have been another person in the vicinity, I thought. If there wasn't then that meant I had killed her. And I had no reason to kill her. For the love of Amir? I wasn't even sure if I liked the guy. I had to finish reading her diary, and mine. I couldn't let this guy take me down to the station tonight. Lt. Lott was waiting for me to respond.

"Did you find the murder weapon?" I asked.

"No. But we're looking."

I forced another phony smile. "Well, I can't help you in that department."

"What were you wearing last night, Jenny?" he asked suddenly.

I shrugged. "I don't know. A pair of jeans and a top."

"May I see those clothes?"

"Right now?"

"Yes. You haven't washed them, have you?"

"No. I just have to think exactly which ones they are." I shook my head. "I can't remember. But you're welcome to go through my clothes before you leave."

"The court has already given me that authority," Lt. Lott said.

"He's already been in your room," my mother said quietly. "And gone through your things."

I was annoyed. "Did you find any bloody clothes?" I snapped at him.

"No. But I wasn't surprised. Now that you're home, I'll have to examine the trunk of your car."

I shrugged. "Go right ahead."

Lt. Lott took out his notepad and studied it. "I have been trying to verify the things you've already told me. What amazes me is that, even in the most elementary respects, your answers were faulty."

"Lieutenant," my mother interrupted. "I am a physician and am well aware of the effects of shock on both the mind and body. I am sure in your profession you must also know how it can throw a person into an incoherent state. It is my understanding that you questioned my daughter immediately after telling her that her best friend had been murdered. Is that correct?"

"Yes, it is, Mrs. Hobbs."

"Then what would you expect?" my mother asked. "That her answers would be given with pinpoint accuracy?"

Lt. Lott held up his hand. "I understand your argument. I'm sure in the days to come I will hear it again and again. But you are right to say I have experience with shock victims. That is why I can state, without any personal reservations, that Jenny did not go into shock when I told her about Crystal's death. She exhibited none of the classic signs. Furthermore, when I told her about her friend's murder, she wasn't even surprised."

"Yes, I was," I protested.

"Not really," Lt. Lott said. "For the most part your reaction was very mild. I was surprised."

"But you're not surprised now?" I asked.

"No."

"Because you think I murdered her?" I asked.

"That's correct."

"Oh God," my mother whispered.

I forced another strained laugh. "How did I murder her? Did I just whip out a knife and start hacking away? Just because, after almost two decades, she had finally ticked me off?"

"Crystal was stabbed many times," Lt. Lott said.

"This is ridiculous!" I cried. "I don't have the strength to kill her! And she wouldn't have stood still while I knifed her over and over."

"If you took her by surprise," Lt. Lott explained patiently, "you would only need to stab her once deeply to render her vulnerable to subsequent stabs." He added, "And from what we can surmise, she was taken by surprise. That is not to say she didn't fight back." He nodded to my bandaged right hand. "How did you say you got those cuts?"

I stiffened. "On a broken glass."

"Where is this broken glass?"

"I threw it out."

"Where is the garbage bag you put the glass in?"

"You asked me that this afternoon. I told you, I don't know."

"You said 'I don't know' and that you couldn't remember many times this afternoon. To the

most basic of questions, you gave evasive answers. You couldn't remember your boyfriend's
last name. You couldn't even remember how long
you had been dating."

"But that should tell you that my daughter *was*
in shock," my mother said. "Why would Jenny
lie about things that have absolutely nothing to
do with Crystal's death?"

Lt. Lott was silent a moment, studying me. "I
don't know. And it bothers me. Yet the facts of
the case remain. Jenny was the last person seen
with Crystal, and there is strong physical evidence that she was present at the scene of the
crime."

"But you have offered no motive for this
crime," my mother argued. "You can speak to
anyone in town. Crystal and Jenny were as close
as two people not intimately-involved can be."

Lt. Lott continued to stare at me. A faint smile
touched his lips, but I wouldn't say it was a happy
smile. He had not lied earlier when he said he
took no pleasure in any of this.

"Do you have a motive for this crime?" he
asked me.

I met his gaze. "No."

"You don't want to tell your mother about
your physical relationship with Amir?"

Beside me, my mother gasped. I patted her
hand, although I continued to focus on the

detective. "I have nothing to hide. We're friends, that's all."

"That's not what he says," Lt. Lott replied. "He told me that you've had sexual intercourse on at least two occasions in the last two weeks."

I snorted. "Gimme a break."

"Are you indicating that you never slept with him?" he asked.

"That's exactly what I'm saying. Why would you take his word about this?"

"Because he has an alibi for the time Crystal was murdered. Because his hairs were not found at the scene of the crime. Because we have no evidence his car was there. Because I was able to test the accuracy of everything else he told me." Lt. Lott paused. "You say he is your friend. Why would he lie about the nature of your relationship?"

"I don't know. Why don't you ask him?"

"That's a feeble response," Lt. Lott said.

I was silent. He was right. My mother stirred beside me.

"Did you sleep with Amir?" she asked softly.

I looked straight ahead. "No. I would remember if I had."

"Why did you lie about Amir's and Mitch's feelings for each other?" Lt. Lott asked.

"I didn't lie."

"But they despise each other. You must have known that."

"If they despise each other, they've kept it hidden from me."

Lt. Lott sighed and shook his head. "I want to help you, Jenny. Honestly I do. But you're going to have to help me. You're going to have to stop giving these evasive answers." He paused. "What happened last night?"

I stared at the far wall. "I don't remember."

"When did you last see Crystal?"

"I don't remember."

"Did you kill her?"

"I don't . . ." My voice trailed off into nothing. I stopped to look at my mother, the detective, my own hands. There was no blood on my hands, no hate in my soul. Had I committed such an atrocious act, I thought, there would be some kind of festering inside me. But my pain was caused by grief alone, for people I no longer knew. For myself as well as Crystal.

"Jenny?" Lt. Lott said gently.

My eyes burned with unshed tears. I couldn't drop my defiant attitude. It was all I had left that belonged to me. Just my words, spoken in a voice that my little brother said sounded different.

"No," I said. "I didn't kill her. I loved her. You don't kill someone you love. That's the simple truth, and if you don't believe me, then I don't know what to say."

"If you didn't kill her," Lt. Lott said, "then who did?"

I hesitated, feeling a peculiar sense of déjà vu. It wasn't as if I had lived this moment before. It was more as if I had *viewed* it before, but from a great distance. From the stars even, a place in the black sky where fates crossed and destinies collided. The detective's question touched me in a profound manner. All signs did point to me, of course. It had been designed that way. From the beginning.

"Whoever killed her," I said quietly, "hated me as much as Crystal."

"Why do you say that?" Lt. Lott asked.

"Because I know this person," I heard myself say. I was still far away, in the past, or the near future. That's where my dreams were from, I realized. They were not of this dimension. I added, "I just don't know his name."

CHAPTER 13

LT. LOTT FINALLY LEFT, BUT NOT WITHOUT SEARCH-ing through my room and car for over an hour. His inspection was thorough; he did it wearing plastic gloves so he wouldn't contaminate any evidence. He took a lot of my clothes, including the sweats I had changed into after reaching my car. Seeing the sweats go into one of his plastic bags, my heart skipped a beat in my chest. They would examine the material under a microscope, I realized, and find the blood drops I had missed. Maybe, though, the bleach had destroyed any usable remains.

He made me remove my bandages. He photographed the cuts.

They did look like scratches. Even the deep one.

My mother followed all this with haunted eyes. She had begun to look at me differently.

My own mother. But I didn't take it personally.

I didn't know what my personality was.

Lt. Lott did not leave without issuing a final warning. He'd be back in the morning, he said. I was not to leave the house. A police officer would be stationed across the street all night to make sure I didn't leave. And when he did return, it would be to arrest me. Tonight would be the last night I could sleep in my own bed. My mother saw him out.

Mom and I—well, we didn't have a lot to say to each other, right then. I retired to my room as quickly as possible. The last thing I saw my mother do was remove a jar of sleeping pills from her black bag. Mother's Little Helpers. I supposed she wouldn't get to sleep without them.

I waited in my room fifteen minutes before I peeked in on Gator. He was pretending to be asleep under the blankets, with the lights out. But, of course, he was wide awake, excited to tell me about his adventures. I turned on the lamp beside his bed and sat next to him. He was glowing. He was fit to be a spy. Before saying a word, he pulled out Crystal's diary from under his pillow and handed it to me.

"I stole it," he said, hardly able to contain his glee.

I had to smile. "Good boy. Did you have any trouble?"

"No. They weren't home. I was in and out of there in one minute flat." He paused and nodded at the diary. "Does it say in there who killed Crystal?"

"It might," I replied, holding it to my chest.

"Then you can show it to the police and they'll leave you alone?"

"Actually, I don't think it will be that simple. Clues to the killer's identity might be in here, but it may be that only I'll be able to recognize them."

He nodded. "I understand." But he didn't look like he did.

I reached over and hugged him. "Thanks, Gator. I owe you."

"What are you going to do now?"

"Study this diary." And my own. But I didn't want to tell him that.

Gator looked suddenly worried. "I'm going to see you in the morning, ain't I?"

"Sure," I said. But the word was no sooner past my lips when I felt how wrong it was. This was it,

I thought. I was not going to see my little brother ever again. Yet that also didn't feel right. There was a mystery here that intuition and dreams could not solve. Yet without a past, they were almost all I had to go on. Gator continued to watch me anxiously. I had to say something more, something that was not only true, but also made sense to both of us. For some reason, I was reminded of the robot character he was always talking about. I asked what his name was again.

"Clyde," Gator replied. "He's a good robot."

"I'm sure he is. You remember how you told me last night that he'd died? But that he might be back next week?"

"Yeah. If they can fix his positronic brain, he should be all right. But you never know. The positronic pathways are very delicate. He might come back to life but not be the same."

Again, I had to laugh. "Well, your sister is a bit like Clyde. My positronic pathways got scrambled somehow. That's why I'm having trouble remembering things. But that doesn't mean I'm done for. I can be fixed." I paused. The words that came out of my mouth next seemed to emerge from a place beyond thought and reason. Yet they rang with truth. I just felt like I had to say them before they choked inside. Before it was too late. "Gator," I whispered softly, with feeling.

He was sensitive to my state. "Yes, Jen?"

"I love you."

He beamed, although he was still scared. "I love you, too. I don't want anything to happen to you."

I sighed. "That's what I want to tell you. If anything should happen to me, it doesn't mean that I'm gone. That I've left you. Like Clyde, when all seems completely lost, I can still come back. It's true I may not be exactly the same. I might even talk different, and you might have trouble recognizing me. But I'll still be Jenny, and you'll still be my brother. Do you understand?"

He struggled. "I think so."

I hugged him again, so hard I might have hurt his bony body. "It doesn't matter. Whatever happens, we just have to trust that it happens for a reason. That in the end, everything will be all right. I believe that. Do you?"

He let go of me and nodded vigorously. "I think you and Clyde will both win in the end," he said.

"That's right," I agreed. "We're going to win."

There were only three entries in Crystal's diary after the last one I had read, which had been dated Nov. 12th. Everything I was about to read was recent, since today's date was Nov. 23rd.

Nov. 14th

I am dating Dr. Jekyll and Mr. Hyde. In the last couple of days, Amir has gone from a sweet and loving young man to a cold, cruel zombie. Yet it is not that simple, either, because signs of the old Amir are still there. I don't know what's set him off, or why he's changed so much. But I have my suspicions.

The day after I almost slept over, I went to see him. It was after school and I swung by without calling, which he told me never to do. But I decided he'd be happy to see me. I found him smoking hashish and reading a gun magazine. When I walked in, he just stared at me like I was a total stranger. I mean, I suspected he did drugs. I was pretty sure, in fact. Several times before, when we were out, he seemed slightly intoxicated. I didn't approve, but I thought it was just a bad habit he'd picked up from home. I thought he'd stop as he got used to living here, to being with me. When I walked in, I didn't flip out because he was getting high—it was because of the look he gave me, like I had just broken into his house and stolen his family treasures. Without giving me a chance to speak, he told me to get out. To leave and never come back.

I left. But I went back three hours later.

I figured he'd be sober by then, and apologize.

And at first he did act apologetic, like he'd been a complete fool. He apologized a half dozen times. I forgave him, of course, what else was I supposed to do? I love him. He wanted to make love and started kissing me. But he was too aggressive, and I didn't feel comfortable. I told him that maybe we should wait till later. But he said he had to have me right then. He needed to feel part of me. So we undressed and got into bed and . . .

It was awful. I felt like I'd been raped. Physically, I was sore, and emotionally I was a wreck. All the right words were coming out of his mouth but it was like I was just a thing he was using quickly, so he could be done with me. When we were finished, he picked up his gun magazine and asked me to leave. I was crying, but he didn't seem to care. He reached for his pipe, his hashish. He told me if I did stay, I had to get stoned with him.

So I left. I don't know if I'm ever going back.

But I still love him. I don't know what to do.

I wish I could talk to Jenny about this.

"Why couldn't you talk to me about it?" I said out loud to the book. Were we close only on the surface? It made me sad to think that Crystal couldn't trust me in a moment of crisis. I prayed I had nothing to do with Amir's abusive behavior. What were Crystal's suspicions?

I continued on to the next page.

Nov. 15th

I saw Amir tonight. I'm so pathetic—I went to see him again. But this time I called first. On the phone, he sounded better, happy to hear from me. When I was there in person, though, it was another story.

We had a "talk." I suppose all couples at one time or another have these talks. It was my turn to do some shouting and crying. He got angry a couple of times but he never raised his voice. Thank God for small favors. Mrs. O'Bannon saw me on the way out and it looked as if she knew everything that had happened. But she's a good woman, and it's not her fault if she could hear my shouting.

Anyway, the bottom line for him is that I am not good enough for him anymore. He needs someone who excites him. He said he had dreams and fantasies about me, but I wasn't living up to them. I asked him, I begged him, what I could do to make him happy. But he just laughed and said there was nothing in this world that I could do. He needed a goddess and I was just an earthly woman. Like, that's fair to me, right?

Why didn't I just walk away right then?

Why did I beg to make love to him one last time?

All my love—it didn't impress him. Leaving, I felt like a tramp. He was already lighting his hash pipe. But then he had the nerve to ask me a favor. He said, finally, he would be happy to meet Jenny. Feeling absolutely miserable, I just shook my head and said it wasn't going to happen. But then he jumped up and grabbed my arm, kind of hard, and leaned over and whispered in my ear.

"Yes," he said. "I think it's time the three of us got together."

I don't know what the hell he thinks will happen.

I only know I don't want to be any part of it.

He's a bastard. Why do I still miss him?

There was only one entry left. It was dated six days ago.

Nov. 17th

I'm afraid. I feel as if my whole life is exploding. The world has gone insane. Everybody is a stranger. I don't know anyone anymore. I don't know myself.

Trauma number one. And I started it.

I was in Baker last night. I went there to see a movie, by myself. I just felt I needed to get away. But who did I run into but Mitch. Get this, he's not with Kathy Kahn but Samantha Beck, Miss Pretty Pom-Pom herself. They're in the back row, rolling around in the seats like they're in a haystack. I swear, that guy's got no class. The movie was only rated PG. Most of the audience was kids. But those kids just had to look over their shoulders to get the coming attractions. What it's like to be a senior in high school. A stud football jock with the IQ of a goal post.

I couldn't stand it. I mean, this guy is supposed to be going with my best friend. He's constantly taking money from Jenny to pay for his gambling debts. Grabbing my Coke and popcorn I stormed over to them. Without saying a word, I threw my drink all over Mitch. Got Samantha, too. Her makeup streamed down her face and she looked like a grotesque Halloween mask. I had to laugh—

until Mitch leapt up and grabbed me by the throat.

"Outside," he snapped.

He dragged me outside. The ushers didn't stop him. I didn't blame them. Mitch is a pretty big guy. Yet I didn't feel in any danger, not at first. What could he do to me? But when we were outside he got vicious. Ten times worse than Amir on a bad hash day. He let go of my throat but not my arm. He had a big fat finger in my face the whole time he shouted at me.

"You sonofabitch," he swore. "You think you're so pure and polished. You think you have the right to judge me? I'll tell you something, Crystal, you're no better than the rest of us. The whole school knows you're doing it with that greasy Egyptian."

"Amir is my boyfriend! Jenny is supposed to be your girlfriend!"

"That's right! And don't you forget that. Jenny is my girlfriend until I decide she isn't. You don't tell her what you saw here to-night."

I laughed in his face. "You've got to be kidding me! The first thing I'm doing when I get back to Carlsrue is tell her! I should have spoken to her when I saw you with Kathy

153

Kahn. But I thought that was just a one-time mistake. Now I see you're a fake from your hairy toes to your fat head."

He slapped me then. Not hard enough to leave a lasting mark, but hard enough to snap my head back. The blow caught me completely by surprise. I mean, I cheer for this guy at football games. He put his fat finger right up to my nose. His eyes were like slits into a furnace.

"You listen, Crystal, and you listen good," he said. "You don't mess with me, I don't mess with you. But you cross me—you go to Jenny with what you saw here tonight—and you're going to pay the price. You get my meaning?"

I sneered. "What are you going to do? Hit me again? You big stinking gorilla. You have no right to tell me what to do. You have no right to even look at my best friend. I'll tell her what I decide to tell her."

He let go of me then, slowly, but his eyes continued to bore into mine. He scraped the nail of his fat finger along the base of my throat, and he smiled as he did it, like he'd just had a great idea, a funny idea that I couldn't imagine.

"You do that then," he said quietly. "You

do what you think is best. And we'll see how far it gets you."

Mitch. What a guy.

And I was the one who told Jenny to invite him to the Sadie Hawkins dance.

Trauma two.

When I got back to Carlsrue, I didn't talk to Jenny. I was too upset. I wanted to speak to her when I'd cooled off, explain exactly what had happened without embellishing the facts. I know Jenny thinks I exaggerate. So I went into my bedroom to go to bed. I went to sleep, I think.

I had that dream again, about that guy and that woman in the Middle East. I would assume I was dreaming about Amir, but it's not clear. I never see the guy's face. Actually, in the dream, I am always the guy. But, like I said before, this guy might be a girl for all I know. He or she is cruel.

This time I was on top of a hill with the old witchy woman. There were statues of demons and other weird characters all around us. It was night and the moon was bright. In the distance I could see the pyramids, but it wasn't like they were monuments from an ancient past. Maybe it was because I was stoned in the dream, but the pyramids looked *alive. Like they were vibrating with light, sending out secret signals to alien creatures in deep space. Hey, we're over here. Land here, and take us away. We're sick of this planet. I had all kinds of weird thoughts running through my head.*

This time the old woman was trying to explain important things to me, but I wouldn't listen. So she got mad and tried to run away. But I didn't like that either. I grabbed her, and made her tell me everything she knew. Then when she was done I took out my knife and held it to her throat. That was the really horrible part. Because she begged me not to hurt her and I kept laughing and cutting her a little bit, each time a bit deeper, until the front of her robe was covered with blood. I showed her no mercy, although none of my cuts went that deep. I was just torturing her. I knew I wasn't going to let her go. . . .

God, it got so bloody after that. I took the knife and—

Wait a second. Someone is calling. Odd, it's the middle of the night. I'll be back in a minute. I just have to write down all this nightmare, and purge it from my soul. It feels like an alien growing inside me.

Crystal's diary ended there. The remainder of the pages were blank. Perhaps it was Mitch who called her, maybe Amir. Naturally, I couldn't remember having called her.

So Mitch threatened to kill her. Interesting.

I bet Lt. Lott didn't know that.

But how would science explain the phenomenon of two close friends having an identical dream, unknown to each other? I did not believe it could. But the alternative was even harder to believe.

We were dealing with some kind of supernatural force.

I reached for my diary, thumbed through the pages. Like Crystal, in the last month, I had only three entries that were recent. The first was from five days ago, the day after Crystal's last entry. I read it with great interest. It was curious how we dated our entries exactly the same. Even our writing styles were very similar.

Nov. 18th

I met Amir today! He came over to my house. Crystal brought him. He is amazing, truly. His face is so intense, so sensual—I had trouble taking my eyes off him. Being with him was powerful. Yet, at the same time, he looked familiar. I could swear I had met him before, somewhere.

Crystal didn't stay for long. She had to get to work. I offered to drive Amir home, so we could have a chance to spend some time together, get to know each other better. Crystal didn't appreciate the offer. She didn't look good, to be frank. There were dark circles under her eyes and she couldn't sit still. Actually, I wondered how the two of them were getting along. She said everything was fine but the way they related to each other— it wasn't the way two people in love should act in each other's company.

Eventually Crystal did leave and Amir and I got to have a great talk. He's interested in many of the things I am: diving, astronomy, history, archaeology. He told me about the fabulous ruins they have in Egypt, how he could feel the past just by sitting in them, late at night. Like myself, Amir is a vampire. He never goes to sleep until after three in the morning. Boy, he must have trouble with Crystal, who likes to be in bed by ten.

After a while Gator came home. Maybe it was good. We would have just kept talking, and then I would have been late to work. I told Amir I'd drive him home, like I promised Crystal. He was very quiet in the car. I wondered if it was because he was embar-

*rassed about where he lives, which is a real
hole in the wall. But just as he got out of my
car, he leaned over and kissed my cheek. It
was a friendly kiss, but it got me thinking
more than friendly thoughts. I know Crystal
would die if she read this but I wish—just
sort of, kind of—that they weren't involved.
Then I could go out with him. Go all the way
out on a limb with him. I bet he's an extraor-
dinary lover.*

*He smiled and told me he hoped to see me
soon.*

*I just grinned. I was too busy blushing to
speak.*

I could see that I wasn't losing any sleep over
Mitch. Nor was I above flirting with my best
friend's boyfriend. Obviously loyalty wasn't one
of my strong points. Couldn't I see how Crystal
was suffering over Amir? Was I that blind? I was
sure Lt. Lott would have enjoyed this last entry.
Perhaps one day it would be read aloud to a jury.
The court will note what a slut Jennifer Hobbs
was. I made a vow to burn the book before the
detective came for me in the morning.

I had known Amir less than a week. What a liar
he was.

But why had he told such an obvious lie?
Was *his* memory defective?

The next entry was two days later, three days ago.

Nov. 20th

What a night. What a disastrous night. I don't see how it could have been worse. Maybe if an asteroid had hit the earth in the middle of it, yeah. Earthquakes and tidal waves could have made it worse. But not much else.

I was working the late shift at Denny's. Mitch came by to see me. He needed money. He always needs money. He must owe me fifteen-hundred dollars. I'm never going to see it. I don't know why I continue to see him. Really, honestly, I swear, it's going to end in a few days. Maybe sooner.

I was supposed to get off at one. Mitch came in at twelve, and milked our coffee pot till he had a gallon of caffeine bubbling in his veins. He got strung out. He couldn't sit still in a booth. He kept bouncing over to the phone, the toilet, the newspaper rack. Ten times he asked me if I was almost finished. I told him to look at the clock. It doesn't lie.

A quarter to one, Crystal comes in with Amir. I hadn't seen her up so late in years. She looked hung over, as if from lack of sleep or a bad argument. Both can do it to you, I

*should know. But Amir was shining. He was
so cool, the way he strode in, moving like he
owned the joint, the entire planet—I wanted
to give him a hug. They joined Mitch in his
booth. I told them I got off in a few minutes,
but Amir said he was hungry so I took his
order. Bacon and eggs and toast. I didn't
know they ate bacon in Egypt. But what the
hell do I know? I put his order in and went to
wait on another table. Then while I was
preparing a bill, Mitch snapped his finger—
the way he always does—loud. He wanted
more coffee. Like his hyperactive bladder
needed another refill. I went for the pot.*

*The next thing I heard was shouting.
Mitch was yelling at Amir. Seemed Amir
didn't like the way Mitch ordered me around,
and he had the balls to tell Mitch so. Of
course Mr. Quarterback of the Year loved
having his behavior corrected. Mitch was on
Amir in a second, but he'd picked the wrong
guy to mess with. They know how to defend
themselves in the Middle East, all those wars
and plagues of locusts. Mitch jumped up and
drew his fist back to punch out Amir. He
ended up missing by two feet. Amir ducked,
and then twirled Mitch around with a
blindingly fast martial arts move. Before he
knew it, Mitch had his right arm pinned*

behind his back at an awkward angle. All this time Crystal was screaming her head off for them to stop. I ran over just as Amir asked for Mitch's surrender. But good old Mitch, fair fighter that he is, grabbed a knife off the table. Thankfully it was a butter knife, but it still must have hurt when he stabbed it into Amir's leg. Amir didn't like that. He kicked Mitch so hard behind the right knee that I swear I heard cartilage pop. Mitch hit the floor hard, cursing like a fiend.

Officer Jakes came in right then for a cup of coffee.

He had no trouble getting the boys to kiss and make up.

Mitch stormed out. Amir just laughed it all off.

I love a boy who sees the humor in every situation.

What disturbed me most about this last entry, besides the obvious violence, was my reaction to it. I seemed to take it all in stride, as if it were just another night at Denny's. Indeed, Amir's self-defense abilities seemed to turn me on. I didn't appear to be worried that Crystal was going through a difficult time. I didn't stop to ask myself what was causing it. No wonder she didn't confide in me when things were rough. I wasn't there for her. I was already plotting the ruin of what was left of her relationship with Amir.

What a coincidence that Mitch spontaneously went for the knife.

There was one more entry. Two days ago.

The day before the murder of Crystal Denger.

Nov. 21st

Amir kissed me today. I don't know what to say. He kissed me on the lips, not on the cheek. He kissed me long and hard so I must have kissed him back. I hardly remember the details. Just the overwhelming sensation.

I feel guilty. I feel horrible. I feel so turned on I think I am going to do something I know I shouldn't do. Crystal would die if she knew what I'm contemplating.

I left school early today, after chemistry. I had to start work at one and I needed to wash and iron my uniform. Besides, I didn't mind missing art and PE. I was in the house only ten minutes when I realized Amir was standing behind me. I hadn't heard him come in. Certainly I hadn't heard him knock. I told him as much, trying to sound annoyed. But then he walked over and started kissing me. Maybe that's the way they do it in Egypt.

Conversation is not a premium item. Maybe that's the way they should do it here. I felt his hands all over me. I'm not sure where they went, but I didn't mind that's for sure.

I am a total slut. I hate myself. I deserve to die.

He didn't stay long, thank God. But he wants me to come over to his place tomorrow, at the same time, one. Shaking my head, I told him I couldn't possibly, but he just laughed at me. He knew, he knows, I will be there. But is he right? I can't do this to Crystal. I mustn't do this to her. I love her. I don't love Amir.

I just want to screw him is all.

More than anything in the whole universe.

His hold over me is almost mystical.

I feel I need him to be complete. Nothing else can be substituted.

Perhaps because of all the excitement and guilt, I have a splitting headache right now. I feel as if the two hemispheres of my brain are at war. I haven't been sleeping well the last few nights. I keep having bloody dreams, which I can hardly remember when I wake up. All I know is that they scare me.

All I know is that I want him.

Want to be scared.

My diary ended. The rest of the smooth vanilla pages were untouched. My questions were left unfulfilled and unanswered. Did I or didn't I? Amir said I did, but he was a proven liar. Yet I couldn't condemn him because I was no better.

God how I hated this life I had forgotten. This superficial Jennifer Hobbs who traded love and devotion for lust and desire. So easily, too, it seemed. Just, I've got to have him and so I will have him. If Crystal hadn't been stabbed in the heart, her heart would have been broken anyway when she found out the truth. And she would have found it out, in the end.

Tonight might be the end for me.

But what was I going to do, now that I knew everything there was to know about the private lives of the two bodies that lay for hours last night beside the cold clear pond? I still didn't know who the murderer was. I hadn't even been able to eliminate myself from the suspect list. But perhaps I had given myself a hint as to who the real killer was with my last few remarks.

Want to be scared.

In what was perhaps a Freudian slip, I had tied Amir into my dreams. Linked him to the blood by linking my headaches to my fear. Yes, I had dreamed the inexplicable nightmares before I had lost my memory. Perhaps if I slept now, and returned to the ancient statues atop the dead hill, another memory would come to me. The moon had been full last night as well as in the haunted dream.

My plan then, to save myself, was to go to bed.

Unlike my mother, I fell asleep quickly without pills.

It was as if oblivion waited for me.

CHAPTER 14

I LEANED OVER AND SPOKE SOFTLY IN HER EAR. "TELL me."

The blood from where I had scratched her throat with my knife continued to trickle down the front of her black robe. Seen in the stark white light of the blazing moon, the dark fluid glowed with an almost radioactive energy. It was as if her life essence were departing her body as I held her pinned with the tip of my blade. She continued to stare at me, this ugly old woman— my mother—whom I had cursed since the day I learned to speak. She was afraid, yes, but she didn't believe I'd kill her—not her own son. She knew so little about me.

"You don't deserve to know," she repeated.

"None of us deserves anything. Still, we take what we can. It is the law of the jungle, and the desert." I gestured to the statues that stood close by. "This is a cemetery. It's a perfect place to leave your body. Few come here, you know."

She sucked in a breath. "Even you would not want the murder of your mother on your conscience."

I laughed. "You amuse me. You talk about conscience when I have seen the soul. What need have I of instruments when I hold the finished product in my hand?"

She hissed. "You have not seen the soul! Your arrogance speaks! You have seen only an illusion."

I nodded. That was the point I was unsure about. The drugs were keys to the past, but jesters in the present, perhaps daggers in the future. I didn't know when the knife in the back could come. She had experience in these matters. Maybe there was one last lesson she could give me.

"That may be true," I said. "Explain this illusion to me. That's all I ask."

She considered. Despite her resolve of a moment ago, she had begun to tremble as my knife probed deeper. "Then you will let me go?" she asked.

"I swear it."

She expressed sarcasm. "You'll swear to anything."

I made her lift her chin by applying more pressure with my knife. "I don't like being called a liar." I nodded to the stone pedestal where she'd been sitting earlier. "Sit down, and I will sit beside you and put my knife away. You will tell me what you know. If I feel you are holding anything back or distorting what you do know—and you understand how sensitive I am to the truth and to lies—I will cut out your heart. But if your explanation pleases me, you will live to see next month's full moon."

She plopped down. "My explanation will not please you," she said bitterly.

I sat by her side, mocked her. "But wise men say the truth is always pleasing to the ear." My knife I hid inside my robe, not far from my hand.

"Wise men do not tread the places you go."

"I turn inside. I seek illumination. My quest is as holy as that of any seeker in the past."

"But you have chosen the dark path. Your insights are temporary. When the drug wears off, you are more deluded than you were before you started."

I shrugged. "You repeat yourself, old woman. The goal is all that matters to me. I take whatever means is quickest." I paused. "Why is my vision of the soul faulty?"

"You have said it yourself. You see this girl, and you can see nothing else. She haunts you night and day. You feel you must find her or you will die."

I nodded. "Yes. That's it exactly. I will never complete my journey without her. I feel she belongs to me, and that I belong to her."

My mother sighed. "That is true. But it is for that very reason you must not go to her."

That angered me. I had to restrain myself from striking her. "But why?"

"Allah does not will it."

I reached for my knife, showed her the blade. "What does Allah will?"

She did not back away. Indeed, a great power entered her voice. Once more the moon flickered in her eyes and I momentarily saw a deity from the past—Isis, the supreme Goddess of light and enlightenment. The one Egyptian deity I feared to swear against. Isis had lived in the hearts and minds of the people when the statues that now peered at us had been created. I didn't think it beyond her power to bring to life one of those statues, and command it to devour me. My mother pointed to the three intertwined demons.

"Do you know what that statue represents?" she asked.

I had never seen such a work of art before. "No," I said cautiously.

"It is symbolic of most human beings who walk in this world."

I had to sneer. "Three fighting demons? How so, old witch?"

"The soul is always one. It can never be otherwise. But the soul cannot incarnate through one body alone. It is too large to be trapped in such a limited cage. You have a name, you have a body. You think that is who you are." She raised her hand as I began to protest. "True, you have tried to penetrate beyond this most fundamental of all illusions. But you are still bound by it. It is your ego that binds you. You think that you are all that exists of you. But there you are wrong. You are not an individual. No one is, not deep inside where the soul wanders free."

I was confused. "I don't understand. I know I am more than the body and the mind. I have touched my soul. I know it is real."

"You have barely scratched the outer shell of what is real."

My knife was impatient, as was I. "Tell me plainly what you mean."

Her eyes locked on mine. "There are three of each of us. When we are born in this world, it sometimes happens that Allah in his mercy places two parts of our soul together. When that

171

happens there is usually great love, undying friendship. But never does Allah place all three parts together in the same area of the world."

What she was saying fascinated me. It had the ring of profound truth.

"Why not?" I asked.

"Because to do so would be to tempt the ancient gods. Our personalities are like our demons. We have little control over them, and they blot out all but a flicker of our true nature. But if the three parts of our being should come together, prematurely, then madness and death would ensue."

"Why? Tell me why."

"Because the power of the soul bursts forward in an unnatural setting. Above all else, you crave enlightenment, but you have not prepared yourself for it. It is only a life lived in total surrender and service that destroys the ego. It is only when you have left your ego behind that you have a chance to unite with your other aspects. By prematurely bringing together your other parts, you force Allah's hand. And God does not like his hand to be forced."

"Are you saying that this girl I keep seeing is a part of me?"

"Yes. She *is* you. One-third of you. And I sense she has a friend nearby, who is also a part. For the three of you to come together would be a disaster."

"How do you know this other one is near her?"

For an instant the hard lines of my mother's face softened. It was as if she looked at me untainted with the fear and frustration that had become the pattern of her life. I realized, right then, that she had loved me once. But I could not remember having ever cared for her, or anyone.

Except this girl. I could almost taste her love. It would be mine.

"I am your mother," she said softly. "I sometimes know what's in my son's heart."

I shook my head bitterly. "You know nothing of me if you think you are going to prevent me from finding this girl. She is my obsession."

My mother spoke fervently. "And what does obsession have to do with finding the truth? You set out to achieve your goal with the highest intentions. True, you perverted your path with drugs, but at least—as you say—your goal was the same as all genuine seekers. But you have become sidetracked. You moved in the direction of the sun and now you see that more than one planet orbits it. The poisonous combination of your ego and your visions binds you to the darkest of all paths. If you go to this girl, you will have to go to the other. It is inevitable—you will be drawn together like living magnets. Then you will open a black door through which all three demons will crawl. And you will not be able to push them back. You will not have the strength."

I smiled faintly. "That doesn't sound so bad."

My mother scowled. "Even Allah will not be able to help you then. You do not find God by ignoring his most sacred commandment."

Her tone had begun to annoy me again. "Where is this commandment, old woman? I don't see the stone it is written on."

She gestured to the statue of demons. "Do you see the looks of lust and horror on their faces? Is their pain not clear to you?"

"I don't know. It looks like they're having a good time."

"Son—"

"Don't call me that," I interrupted sternly. I had raised my knife blade once more and brought it to rest in the hollow of her throat, which was sticky with drying blood. The wind blew dry from the west. It wouldn't take long for considerably more blood to dry out, I thought, and turn to dust. I wondered if vultures visited this spot.

Nothing she had told me pleased me.

"Never call me that," I said.

Her power left her, her conviction. Fear destroyed all righteousness, in the end. That was why fear was the greatest of all powers, and why I had long ago mastered its use. She trembled as she beheld my inner coldness.

"Fine," she whispered. "I will never call you that again."

I moved closer, brought the tip of my blade to the slick surface of her right eyeball. For an old woman, she had lovely eyes. In their own way, they were penetrating. They had followed me closely all these years. But I had never been fond of spies. Moving carefully and with pleasure, I scratched her eyeball lightly. She tried not to move but her fear shook her. As she blinked, a tear sprang from her eye.

It was a bloody tear.

"Please," she said.

"Please what?"

"I am only trying to save you."

"From what? Myself? Thank you but I don't have a problem with myself. This part or the other two parts. You're right, I am going to see this girl. And if there is another like her, I'll see her as well. I'll have them both, at the same time, and if the black door does break open and the demons crawl through, I'll place them both in front of me as a shield. You see, I may desire them but I don't need them. That is where you have underestimated me. I am more powerful than you can imagine. I don't need you. You do nothing for me now. In fact, there is no reason you should keep on breathing."

Her eyes blazed with fear now, even the bloody one.

"But I'm your mother," she cried.

I tightened my grip on the blade. I began to press harder, into her eye, her head, even into her soul. Right then, I wanted to cut out her heart and hold it up to both Allah and Isis, and show them that no demon frightened me because I *was* a demon.

"But I don't want to be your son," I swore as I began to cut.

The night turned red and full of screams.

It made me laugh.

CHAPTER 15

WHEN I AWOKE, I KNEW HOW CRYSTAL HAD DIED. I also knew that I was innocent. And best of all, I knew how to punish the guilty. But at such a cost . . .

"I can't do it," I whispered to my dark ceiling. But I had to do it. Tonight. Now.

I was going to jail in the morning. For twenty years.

Sitting up in bed, I reached over and turned on the light. For a moment, as the bulb flared to life, the walls of my room looked as if they were splattered with blood. But it was only a lingering impression from my nightmare. The past was another dimension. The visions in my dream world had really happened. He had cut his own mother's eyes out, and enjoyed the task. I had to remember that. My hatred for him would give me strength. But I was also like him, in a way. It would give me pleasure to see him beg.

Getting out of bed, I dressed quickly, in jeans and a sweatshirt. I grabbed my coat. It was eleven-twenty. I'd been asleep about an hour. The time it took for the mother to explain the riddles of the soul to the demon. She should have kept her mouth shut, but I couldn't blame her. Only I understood how terrified she had been.

In the kitchen I found my mother's black doctor bag. Dr. Hobbs obviously made house calls—if you were sick enough. Inside the bag was the jar of sleeping pills my mother had reached for before retiring. Phenobarbital. Fifty soft capsules. Enough to put a young soul permanently to sleep. There was also a smaller container of Valium. The two together would make a potent, if not lethal, combination.

There was also a set of hypodermic needles.

I set those aside, thinking they might be useful.

Peeking out the front window, I saw the cop car parked across the street. The lone officer had his dome light on. I guess they didn't consider me a major threat. The man was reading a book, probably a murder mystery. It was Officer Jakes, my old friend, the one law enforcement official in all of Carlsrue who believed I was innocent. Not that he'd let me just stroll on by him. But at least he would talk to me and take what I had to offer.

I put on a pot of coffee while I searched the drawers and cabinets for rope. I needed something strong, but also something that was easy to cut. I wasn't overly worried about getting trapped. The knife used to kill Crystal had been very sharp.

When the coffee was ready, I poured it into an insulated flask. I mixed in a pinch of sugar, a spot of milk, and the contents of four sleeping capsules. Shaking the flask thoroughly, I made sure all the contents were well blended. It was another cold night. Officer Jakes would welcome a warm drink from the tragically beautiful and falsely accused Jennifer Hobbs.

I left the rope inside as I went out to visit him. The rope was for later.

Officer Jakes looked startled as I approached. He quickly set aside his book and moved to get out of his car. I motioned for him to stay where he was. As he rolled down his window, I held up the flask of coffee.

"I thought you might need something to keep you warm," I said, handing the flask over. "I guarantee you, it's better than Denny's."

"Thanks, Jenny." He immediately poured

himself a cup and held it up in a toast. "To your innocence. May sanity return to the Carlsrue Police Department."

I flashed him a smile. "May it return soon." But then I quieted. "Did you tell Lt. Lott how close Crystal and I were?"

He took a large gulp and nodded. "A thousand times. He wouldn't listen. He thinks he's hot on the trail. He isn't going to get off your case until he runs into a wall." Jakes took another slug. He was obviously thirsty and cold. He shook his head. "The strange thing is, I know Lott. He's a meticulous worker. He's usually dead on with his conclusions, if you'll forgive the pun. I can't understand how he's wandered so far off base by accusing you."

"Is he really going to arrest me in the morning?"

Officer Jakes nodded wearily. "Looks like it. You'd better get hold of a good lawyer and quick. You should never have spoken to us without one. You were upset and obviously couldn't remember what year it was, never mind the exact time you dropped Crystal off or went back out." He paused to have another swallow. He actually emptied his first cup. "The sad thing is that everything you said at that initial interview can and will be used against you."

"Have more coffee. I can always make you

another pot. I don't mind." I added, "But you know I didn't do it, don't you?"

He snorted as he poured himself another cup. "Jenny. Do you need to ask? Nobody who knew you two could possibly think you murdered Crystal. Why just three days ago my partner Sammy and I saw you and Crystal coming out of the movie theater. We started talking about how real friendship lasts forever. I told Sammy I thought the two of you would still be close when you were seventy years old and had ten grand-children apiece."

I smiled at the thought. "Yeah, Crystal always wanted a lot of kids. She would have made a great mom." I shook my head. "But none of that is going to happen now."

He reached out his window and squeezed my arm. "*You* still have your whole life in front of you. You have to remember that, Jenny. You can't let yourself fall into despair, and let the system walk over you. Tomorrow morning you're going to have to wake up fighting. Lt. Lott wants to close this case fast. If you're not careful, he might slam it shut on top of your head while you're still grieving. Get yourself a lawyer. Get the facts out in the open. That's what will save you."

I nodded weakly. "I know, but I just wish I could sit and quietly mourn Crystal. Instead I have to struggle to explain why I didn't kill her. It's obscene."

Officer Jakes stared up the street and sipped his coffee, looking reflective, maybe a little drowsy. He might have been tired to begin with, so much the better. I figured the drug would take at least twenty minutes to take effect. But perhaps it began to act as a truth serum quicker. I had to remind myself that Officer Jakes was only a few years older than I was.

"I never told you this, Jenny," he said in a soft voice. "But the end of my senior year, when you were a freshman, I was dying to ask you to the prom. You might remember. I kept talking to you at lunch, asking you about everything in the world except whether you wanted to go to the dance with me."

I laughed. "I do remember that! Why didn't you ask me?"

He shook his head. "I didn't have the nerve. I would stand on the other side of the campus and watch you and Crystal together and think, 'There are two of the most beautiful girls in the whole world.' Don't get me wrong. I was only interested in going with you to the prom. But, at the same time, you two were always together. You fit together. You know what I mean? Crystal and Jenny. It was like one word to the rest of us at school."

"It was that way to us, too." It was my turn to touch his shoulder. "I would have gone with you. I would have been honored."

He patted my hand. "Thanks." He paused. "How are you and Mitch doing?"

I snickered. "That creep. We're finished. He came over today asking for money. I kicked him out of the house. He doesn't even care that Crystal's dead."

Officer Jakes nodded seriously. "I'm happy to hear that, even though I know the breakup must be hard on you, especially on top of everything else that's happened. But you're better off in the long run without him. That Mitch is bad news. He's way out on a limb with his gambling debts. The department's investigating him." He added, quickly, "But that's not something we want him to know."

"Don't worry, I won't breathe a word of it to him."

"That's good." He yawned. "I really shouldn't have said anything."

A silence settled between us. I looked down the street, in the direction of I knew not what. Because I didn't know this world. It didn't belong to me anymore. All I had left was my soul, and even that I had to share with a devil.

I stared up at the moon. As far as I could tell, it was full again. I knew it was impossible for it to be a perfect sphere two days in a row. But after seeing it reflected in the clear pond, I knew it would shine on the watery surface like an avenging angel until the heavens were calmed. I had to keep my mind focused on the moon. I couldn't think of anything else that I was doing. *He* might penetrate my plan, and fail to do what must be done. I wished I didn't need his help, but his magic—although black as the demons he worshiped—was the only magic we had.

Officer Jakes took another sip from his cup. "Thanks again for the coffee, Jenny," he said. "You really know how to warm a guy's bones." He stopped to yawn and shook his head suddenly. "I can't believe I just said that. I'm sorry. What I meant is . . ."

"Don't apologize," I interrupted. "I'm not offended. Maybe when this is all over, we can get together sometime." I added, "Maybe you could take me to my prom. Later in the year."

He blinked. All of a sudden his eyes were bothering him. "I'd like that. I'd like that very much."

"Then it's a date," I said, knowing it would never happen. After patting him on the back, I turned toward the house. "You finish your coffee. I'll go make you some more."

"You don't have to," he called.

"It's no problem."

But he was right, he needed nothing more. When I came back outside, I knew he would be sound asleep.

The note was harder to write than I could ever have imagined. I wanted to say so many things, but in the end, for the sake of Crystal's family and my own, all I could do was express my love. If they believed in that, at least, I would have found some peace.

I placed the paper on my bedside table.

After stuffing the rope, hypodermic needles, jars of pills, and keys to my Celica in my coat pockets, I went back outside. Officer Jakes was slumped over on his side behind the wheel of his patrol car, snoring heavily. He looked so cute. Before I reached inside the car to remove his revolver, I kissed him on the cheek.

"Sorry to do this to you," I whispered. "You're a real friend. I don't think Jennifer Hobbs had many of those."

Besides his revolver, I took his shotgun. Both were fully loaded and ready for action. I don't know how, but I knew how to use them. I began to realize there were many ways of knowing.

I stared at the moon as I drove to the park. Digging up the knife, I didn't take my eyes off it. I thought of nothing. It was not hard for me. Now I was nothing, and before the night was finished, I would be even less.

I drove up Highway Seventeen. Into the forest.

It wasn't difficult to find the right place to park. By the side of the road, the gravel had been tossed around. Many police cars had been parked there that afternoon.

Taking my flashlight and climbing out into the brisk Oregon air, I thought of all that had happened in the last twenty-four hours as I walked into the woods. So much pain and confusion. But I let my memory tape run only so far. When I reached the present moment, my eyes returned to the moon. He mustn't know that I had been here now.

I planted the knife beside the tree where Crystal had fallen. The area was roped off with yellow tape, the ground still moist, with blood I think. But I had no problems; I didn't have to hide the knife deep.

Cruising back into town, I decided to swing by Mitch's house. I still had my little black book beside me on the front seat, under the shotgun and revolver. I knew his address. All kinds of devilish ideas started to float around inside my skull.

"The moon," I whispered. "There is only the white light of the moon."

The first time I drove by, I didn't stop or even slow down. A brief glance was all I needed to tell me that Mitch was making out in the front seat of his van with either Kathy Kahn or Samantha Beck or some other unfortunate. He was as rotten a boyfriend as a girl could have. True, I wasn't altogether enamored of the old Jennifer Hobbs, but the new and improved version thought she deserved better.

I swung around the block once more.

But this time I killed my lights and engine. I coasted up behind them without their knowing I was there. Climbing out and cocking the shotgun, I felt like Dirty Harry and Rambo even though I couldn't recall going to a single one of their movies. Moving silently around the side of the van, I raised the shotgun and fired point-blank into the side of it.

The metal exploded.

The young lovers in the front freaked.

I blew out the wheels next, then the radiator and engine. And while they were cowering on the floor and blubbering like babies, I shattered the windshield. The spray of glass as it landed in his hair, I'm sure, must have made him certain that Duke's boys were back for blood. It gave me a feeling of deep satisfaction to hear Mitch praying to Sweet Jesus for protection. The two were in such a state, I was able to drive away without their having the slightest idea who had stopped by to say hi.

My next destination was Amir's apartment.

After quietly climbing the steps to his front door, I knocked softly.

He must have been asleep. Maybe dreaming about the moon goddess.

When he opened the door, he was rubbing his tired eyes.

Poor baby.

I belted him on the side of the head with Officer Jakes's revolver.

He went down hard and I leapt inside, closing the door at my back. Before he could begin to recover, I kicked him in the gut and thrust the pistol against the side of his head. A ray of moonlight stabbed through the parted curtains and I could see he was bleeding from his scalp. The warm red fluid dripped over the black metal of the cold barrel and I saw his fear as well.

It made me want to laugh.

"Amir," I said. "It's Jenny. Want to go for a walk in the woods?"

CHAPTER 16

Off Highway Seventeen, a few miles out of town, we parked in the exact spot I had parked in earlier. It wasn't so hard to drive with one hand, and keep the revolver to his head with the other. He wasn't moving around a whole lot. He still acted dazed and confused. I liked him that way.

"Get out," I said as I killed the engine.

With his hands in the air, he climbed out of my Celica. I followed him through the passenger door, to be on the safe side. He stood with his back to me, the red on his head dark in the moonlight. I hoped I hadn't hurt him too much. I had my reasons. I let him stand there for a moment and drink in the sights. He recovered his voice.

"Why are you doing this to me?" he asked.

"I'm into bondage," I replied. "It turns me on." I nudged him in the back with the tip of the revolver. "On the ground, on your face. Keep your arms spread."

"You'll never get away with this," he said as he dropped to his knees. He hesitated to put his face into the ground, but I gave him a dose of good girlfriend encouragement by shoving the base of his skull with the heel of my foot. With my free hand, I reached into my coat pocket for the jar of sleeping pills.

"I don't know about that," I said. "I'm doing pretty good so far."

He spoke into the mud. "So you really did kill her."

That made me laugh. I got the top off the pills. "Yeah, I killed her all right. I wanted you so bad, I couldn't wait until the two of you broke up. But since then I've gotten tired of you. I'm pretty flaky, huh? Not the most dependable friend. You should worry about that quality in me." I kicked him again in the back of the head as he tried to look around. "You should be worried sick just about now, Amir."

"What are you going to do to me?"

"Make you bleed a little." I reached back into

my Celica for a can of beer I had swiped from Amir's underfed refrigerator. I'd thought of everything. Balancing the gun and the pills and the beer, I slowly began to swallow the phenobarbital. I added, "Maybe make you bleed a lot. It all depends."

"On what?" He sounded scared.

I put another two pills in my mouth and took a hit of beer. "On whether you open your heart to me or not." I added as the pills slid down my throat, "I'm not like your mother. I don't fool myself that I know your darkest thoughts. But I do know a few of them."

He hesitated. "I don't know what you're talking about, Jenny."

"I'm sure you don't. You know I still have the knife."

"You should give it to the police," he said.

"I don't think so. Let me ask you something about it. I'm just curious. Is it the same one?"

"The same one as what?"

"The same one you cut her eyes out with?"

He was a long time answering. "I don't know what you're talking about."

I giggled. "Now you sound like me. For the last twenty-four hours, I've been saying that to everyone. I don't know. I can't remember. But *you* didn't ask me many questions. You were cool about that. You knew it was a waste of time. You knew I couldn't tell you from Adam, or, for that matter, my own mother from Eve." I paused. "But I *know* your mother. I know what you did to her. Tell me the truth, Amir, if you don't want me to start cutting you up now. Is it the same knife?"

He was having trouble breathing. He wasn't such a Big Bad Wolf after all, not when you took away his precious blade. Once more, he tried to get up. This time I kicked his head, right in the wound. Blood flew off my shoe and his scalp. He dropped back down with a thump. Later, I figured, I'd have to pay for the abuse.

"Is it?" I demanded.

He shook in the mud. "Yes," he whispered pitifully. "I brought it with me to this country."

I laughed. I couldn't stop. Maybe it was the pills. Maybe it was my nature, now that the two of us were close again. I would finish the bottle of phenobarbital soon, and then top it off with a few Valium. It was good to get high, to see what was real. Even if it was the dark path.

"That was your first mistake," I told him.

When I finished my medicine, I took a portion of the rope and bound his hands behind his back. It was a good hike from the road to the pond. To hurry him through the trees, I repeatedly had to prod him with the gun. Still, it took us maybe twenty minutes to get there. I didn't have a lot of extra time left for convoluted explanations. But when I finally had him at the spot where Crystal was murdered, I wanted to hear some of the details. Just so I knew. Tying him to the tree beside where Crystal had fallen, I forced him down on his knees. By this time he was trembling visibly. I knelt beside him and put the gun to his cheek.

"Do you smell it?" I asked.

He coughed. "What?"

"That smell. Do you know what it is?"

"No."

"It's her blood. This spot is soaked with it. Stab someone a dozen times and they bleed a lot. But you know that already, don't you? You have experience in these matters."

"Jenny. Don't do this. Let's talk."

I nodded grimly. "We can talk. Tell me how you did it."

"Did what?"

I spoke with scorn. "How you *entered* me. How you raped my mind. How you made me drive my best friend to this forsaken spot. How you made me take your knife and stab it into her body. Again and again." I paused and lowered my voice. "Let's talk about that."

"I don't understand what you mean. I swear it."

"You'll swear to anything." I hardened my

tone as I cocked the revolver. "Pray to Allah, Amir. Pray quick. Your brains are about to explode out of the back of your head."

He wept. "Please, don't! I'll tell you. I'll tell you whatever you want to know. Just promise not to kill me."

I sat back and nodded. "I promise. Talk. Make it good."

He peered at me with his handsome dark eyes. They were bloodshot now. He didn't really believe I would release him, and he was wise in that respect.

"How much do you know?" he croaked.

"I dreamed of you and your mother. I saw and heard all of your last conversation. You took your time killing her." I paused. "You came seeking Crystal. You found her. What was wrong with her?"

"You know how we're all related?"

"Regrettably. I want you to explain more about that as well."

He winced at my words. Or maybe it was the sight of my bloody gun. Not for a second was I turning it away from his face. I stifled a yawn. Now that I was sitting, the effect from the drugs was coming on hard and fast.

"I was ecstatic to find Crystal," he began. "But it hadn't been that difficult to find her, or you, either, for that matter. For a moment here, a second there, I could see through your eyes, through her eyes. This entire area had become familiar to me before I drove into it. But there was also a magnetism at work as I neared you two. It grew stronger and stronger until I felt as if an electric current were flowing through the center of my brain. The current acted like a compass for me. As long as I followed it, I was on the most direct route to Carlsrue. I met Crystal ten minutes after getting here. I just stopped and stared at her. She also stopped and stared. That's how it began. I thought I was in love. I had never felt love before, but this seemed like what love should be. I couldn't stand to be separate from her. I felt I had to possess her, not only her body but her soul."

"Because her soul was your soul," I said. "But you felt even more incomplete in her presence. When you thought you would feel more complete."

He nodded grudgingly. "You have seen deeply, Jenny. I thought when I found her the horrible longing inside would cease. But it only intensified. There is a saying in my country that has been passed down from ancient times. It says that hate is not the opposite of love. Hate is merely love standing upside-down. What it means is that they both arise in the heart. They both stand back to back. They are just different sides of the same coin."

"Your love for Crystal turned to hate?"

He moaned softly. "Yes. And I didn't want that. I didn't plan it. But in the space of one night I found I couldn't stand her. To me she was the most repulsive creature on earth. Yet my longing did not leave me. It was as if I had opened a wound with my devotion to her, but now I had only scorn to soothe it. I felt like I was going out of my mind. I needed to see you. You were the only one who could help me. You were the only one who was like me."

"I was nothing like you," I said bitterly.

He held my gaze. "You *are* me. But if you are referring to our three different personalities, I would say you were more like me than Crystal. I am the demon, no doubt. She was the angel. But you had a little of both of us in you, Jenny. When I finally met you, I thought this would be good. I believed I could balance this power. Honestly, I wanted to love you."

"You just wanted to use me," I snapped. "To please your tormented self."

"Is any other man or woman better? All over the world, people chase after love. It is the preoccupation of the human race. Why? Because people feel incomplete inside. But, imagine, my

196

loneliness was a million times greater than what the average person experiences. I knew what the soul was. I knew it took three bodies each time it incarnated. Can't you see? I alone knew what I was missing."

"And you had to have it," I said, yawning some more. A subtle but all too pervasive dullness was creeping into the back of my brain. Time was not my friend. I continued, "You had to have me. But did you? Tell me the truth, Amir."

He lowered his head. "No. We never made love. We came close, but you wouldn't because of Crystal."

I nodded, relieved. Jennifer Hobbs wasn't a total flake. "Because my love for her was genuine."

"Perhaps. But according to you, I wouldn't know the real thing, would I?"

A rush of hatred poured through me. I came close to hitting him. "According to *me?* Who am I? You took that small thing away, in case you forget. Tell me, by the way, can I get that back? My personality? My memory?"

He looked scared, probably because he knew his answer was not going to please me. "It's gone," he said quietly.

I drew in a breath. *"Where* has it gone?"

He shrugged. "I don't know. Only the soul is permanent. The personality dies with the body."

"But my body is still alive."

"It's gone forever." He paused. "You know that."

Strange, but I did know that. I wouldn't have swallowed so many pills otherwise. Yet his remark brought tears to my eyes. In one sense, I was already as dead as Crystal. In another sense, I was worse off than she had been. At least she left the world knowing who she was. I would never have that chance. All because of this bastard. I cocked the revolver in my hand and leveled the barrel between his eyes.

"I want you to tell me what happened last night," I said softly.

He panted. He really was a coward. "You swore you wouldn't kill me."

"We'll see."

"Jenny—"

"Don't call me that! I am not Jenny! I am no one thanks to you!" I belted him on the side of the head with the gun. The cut on his head continued to bleed. "Talk dammit!"

He spoke rapidly. "You and Crystal came over to my house last night. You were invited, she wasn't. I had been smoking hash half the day. I was gone. I was in that state where I couldn't quite reach the soul but I wasn't in touch with my body either. When the two of you walked in, things just went insane. The demons crawled through the door, as my mother had said. That's a metaphor for the premature rupture of the soul. The power was unbelievable. It shattered all individual barriers. The two of you collapsed writhing on the floor. I was in your body, you were in Crystal's body, she was floating up at the ceiling. Neither of you understood what was happening. But I managed, after great effort, to gain enough control over my own mind to take charge of the situation." He hesitated. "It was then the thought occurred to me."

"To use me to get rid of Crystal?"

He briefly closed his eyes, tried to look repentant for my benefit. "Yes."

I nodded. "The perfect murder. Force your will into another person's body and have that body carry it out. Tell me, did Crystal know what was happening to her at the end?"

He opened his eyes and shook his head. "No. It was a painless death. I swear it."

I smacked him again with the gun. "You lie! I saw her death expression. She died in great pain. In unimaginable horror. You wanted it that way. It gave you joy to witness her suffering. In the end, you let her back in her body so she could feel the knife sinking into her flesh."

He wept. "I didn't want any of this to happen."

I snickered. "Oh, I bet right now you don't." I sat back on my heels, forcing myself to breathe rapidly so I wouldn't pass out. This was the most dangerous juncture, when all could be lost. The tears continued to roll down my face—both sad and bitter—and there was pain in my voice as I spoke. "So you forced your mind into my body. And my mind fell out, into the void, and was lost. Just like that my life was erased."

He nodded weakly. "I don't know where your memory went. If I did, if I could get it back for you, I would."

My vision blurred and I had to steady myself. "Liar. If you could reach this gun you would put a bullet in my brain and walk out of these woods smiling." I tapped the barrel on his forehead. "But you are not going to walk out of these woods, Amir. The police will find your body here tomorrow, and there will be no one in it."

He shuddered. "You won't kill me. You can't kill me. Please!"

"You have a lot of nerve to beg for mercy after what you've done." Still on my knees, I straightened up. I swayed now as if a hard wind were blowing me from the side. I pulled the hypodermic needles from my coat pocket. "You're so into drugs, Amir. You might actually enjoy this. One last stroll down the dark path before you say goodbye to the world."

His eyes blazed with fear. "What are you going to do?"

I took out a needle and plunger, tried to hold it steady in my free hand. "I'm going to inject large amounts of air into your veins. The bubbles will travel through your bloodstream and reach your brain or heart, depending on which vein I use. But either way you will go into horrible convulsions. It will be a much more painful death than a single shot in the head." I paused. "You will experience a portion of the pain Crystal felt when she died. I think that's only fair, don't you?"

I leaned toward him with the needle.

He drew back violently. "Don't! Jenny!"

"Son!" I shouted, enjoying myself. "Don't call me that!"

"Wait!" He tried to crawl around to the other side of the tree, but I had him tied tight. He just ended up tearing at the bark of the tree. "Please! I will tell you a great secret! I will tell you how to get your memory back!"

I snorted. "Give me a break. I may have hardly any mind left, but I'm not going to fall for that one." Again I leaned forward. "Hold still or I'll have to poke out your eyes. And you have such beautiful eyes, like your mother had."

He refused to hold still, but it really didn't matter. I had massive advantages over him. He was tied to a tree and I had the needle and the revolver. After scurrying back and forth around a limited portion of the tree—burning his skin with the rope—he finally began to tire and I was able to get a grip on his neck. Where the big juicy veins were. He screamed for help as my needle slid into his dark sweaty flesh. I thought his cry ironic and told him so.

"But no one can help you now," I said. "You're already a goner."

I went to stab the needle in a second time.

But it fell from my hand. It seemed to fall for a long time. It was as if the needle had become weightless. It floated to earth for a millennium before settling on the blood-stained grass. My vision was strangely altered, expanded and contracted at the same time. Overhead the stars seemed within my grasp, but Amir was receding from me rapidly, as if he were falling down a dark tunnel at the end of which no divine light shone. For him, for now, all was black.

Yet I felt an explosion of white light inside my own being. Throwing my head back, it seemed as if the moon had descended to touch the crown of my skull. For an instant that was burned in eternity, I felt inexplicable power and joy. I was the soul, the eternal being of all creatures, and nothing in this world could contain or command me.

Yet *some* power commanded me. I did not know where the instruction came from, even whether it was benevolent or evil. I only knew I must obey it. I knew I had to reach out and grab Amir's lifeless hands, which I did. The touch would serve as an anchor for me and keep me from losing again what I had already lost at a great price. This time, I believed, the higher power was on my side.

Infinity rushed toward me.

But never reached me.

The moon detonated. In a soundless explosion.

I felt myself fall into the black tunnel where Amir had toppled.

Then I knew nothing. Nothing at all.

A rough hand shook me. Opening my eyes and looking up, I was momentarily surprised to see a pretty young woman with brown hair pointing a revolver at me. She had a nice face but there was something in her eyes that made me nauseous. Kneeling beside me, she grinned wickedly.

"How do you feel?" she asked.

I groaned. "Sick."

Her grin widened. "You almost had me. But there is one thing you forgot about demons." She paused and leaned over and kissed me on the lips, and then whispered in my ear. "We always have something unexpected up our sleeves."

"What are you going to do?" I gasped.

She stood and chuckled. "To you? Nothing.

You've finished the job already." She glanced in the direction of the road. "But I suppose now I will have to get out of town. I pointed all the evidence in your direction, and now it points at me."

I swallowed thickly. "A pity."

She turned away. "Goodbye, Jenny."

I strained to sit up. "Amir?"

She paused. "Yes?"

"I read Crystal's diary. Tonight. She thought you were a lousy lover." I forced a smile. "I just wanted you to know."

She didn't reply, just left in a huff.

I gave her/him a few minutes head start. Then I reached over with my thick masculine fingers and dug at the base of the tree where I had earlier planted the knife. I wasn't worried about air bubbles in my bloodstream because, of course, I had not injected anything so lethal into a body I intended to be hosting soon. I had just stuck the needle in his neck, nothing more. Just wanted to scare him out of his skin, as they say. But Amir hadn't realized that. And here he thought he was so clever. How easily he had fallen for my simple ruse, and used his dark magic to force his way into my body and retake what he believed was the power position. Thank God the cosmos had commanded me to grab his hands. I hadn't thought of that. Despite all my plans, I might have just fallen into the abyss again.

The whole situation struck me as ironic and I laughed.

But what a deep laugh I had!

It was kind of weird not to be a girl anymore, but since that particular female body was, in the eyes of the law, guilty of murder, I didn't mind having undergone such a radical cosmetic change. In a way it would have been fun to leave him alive inside my old body, to see him rant and rave about his innocence. Then again, that could be dangerous. Who knew what mischief he could get into, even in jail. Better the pills did their work and it ended tonight. While the moon was just a shade past full.

Finding the knife, I cut myself free and headed back toward the car. I was surprised to find he had gotten as far as the vehicle with so many drugs in his system. My old body sat slumped behind the wheel of the Celica, the keys in the ignition, the engine silent. I wondered what his last thought had been as he fell asleep.

Probably surprise.

I drove us both home. My body continued to live, to breathe, but it was only a matter of time now. The breathing was very shallow.

At the house I was relieved to see that Officer

Jakes was still unconscious. After parking in the driveway, I lifted Jennifer Hobbs's body from the passenger seat and carried it inside. Gator and my mother continued to rest undisturbed. Undressing my old form, I slipped it beneath the blankets and sat beside it for a long time, feeling many emotions: a relief as profound as my sorrow, a cold pain as gentle as a warm caress. They were all there, inside.

It was over, true, but in a way God usually never allowed it to be over. That was both good and bad. We were *all* both good and bad. That was the lesson of our tale. Our only chance at enlightenment was to balance our conflicting natures. The darkness was as much a part of us as the light. I believed I would miss Amir as much as I missed Crystal. In a sense, I had known him better. The devil always speaks louder than the angel.

I was not tempted to reach out and smother the last breaths.

I just waited. There was time.

I placed the bottle of pills next to my suicide note.

But the knife I kept for my own.

Close to the time I had woken up beside the pool twenty-four hours earlier, Jennifer Hobbs's body let go of its last breath. The chest no longer moved. I didn't have to close the eyes. They were already closed. I hoped the mind behind them was finally at peace.

I stood and, collecting the two diaries, left the house.

I washed the revolver off, outside under the faucet. Placing both guns back where they belonged, I stretched a blanket over still-sleeping Officer Jakes and once again kissed him on the cheek.

"Don't grieve for me," I whispered.

I walked home. To my new home.

EPILOGUE

THE FUNERAL FOR CRYSTAL DENGER AND JENNIFER Hobbs was held four days after Crystal's murder and three days after Jennifer's apparent suicide. It was a joint service and it was later estimated that one quarter of the town turned out to pay their last respects. Both Crystal and Jennifer had been born and raised in Carlsrue, and small towns both celebrate and grieve together much like large families. It was, as the local pastor said at the funeral, as if they had all lost two daughters. No one understood why Jennifer had done what she had, but no one wanted to blame her. There was too much sorrow for pointing fingers.

But maybe that would change later, human nature being what it was.

I attended the funeral and stood beside both families, feeling more out of place than any of them could have imagined. Lt. Lott was also present, as was Officer Jakes. They stood at opposite ends of the caskets; perhaps their positioning said it all. But the detective, to his credit, wore only genuine grief on his face. He had caught his murderer, he thought, but justice had not prevailed.

Little did he know that the exact reverse was true.

When the pastor had finished talking, and flower petals had been sprinkled over the caskets, along with many tears, I walked Mrs. Hobbs down the grassy knoll and around the gravestones to her car. Like myself, she was dressed in black, and the pain etched in her face was something I would have given my life to erase. But I had given my life for other things, I thought, and that was why my mother was burying her daughter today. So *she* thought. But there was no point in trying to tell her otherwise. With shaking hands, she pulled a folded paper from her bag as she was getting in her car.

"This is her note," she said. "The police and Crystal's parents have seen it. No one else." She added without judgment, "I know you were close to her. I thought you would want to read it."

I spoke firmly. "Jenny was my friend, nothing more."

"But I thought you told the detective—"

"I told him nothing," I interrupted as I took the paper. Of course, there was no need for me to read what I had written. But I did anyway, for my mother's sake.

> To my family, Crystal's family, and my friends,
>
> I did not kill Crystal. I realize that when my body is found, my suicide will be proof to everyone of my guilt. But nothing could be further from the truth. I give my life now to stop Crystal's true murderer, to prevent him from murdering again. Even as I write these words, I know they will never be understood. But I write them anyway because they are true.
>
> I loved Crystal more than life itself. I would never have harmed her. I pray her life, and my own, and the love we shared together is what is remembered by those who loved us. What has happened during these last twenty-four hours is just illusion and madness. My only regret,

as I leave, is that it will never be forgotten.

Gator is the greatest little brother in the world.

                                        Jenny

"I believe her," I said as I finished reading.

My mother was confused. "What do you believe? She swallowed all those pills and . . ." Her pain was too much. She had to stop to take a breath. With tears in her eyes, she looked up at the sky. She spoke almost as if she were praying. "I don't understand. Jenny would never have done these things. Never."

I patted the woman on the back. "That's what I mean. I believe her. I hope you can believe her, too."

It was too hard for her to continue speaking. My mother wiped away a tear, nodded sadly, and climbed into her car. It was only then we both realized she had forgotten Gator. I saw the small boy still up at the grave site. Telling my mother to wait a moment, I jogged back up the grassy slope. He stood uncertainly beside his sister's casket, a small hand on the wooden box. He didn't know what he was doing, he just didn't want to leave her. I knelt by his side.

"Gator," I said gently. "Your mother's waiting for you."

He looked over, his innocent face hurt beyond his years. Yet a trace of surprise touched his cheeks. "You've never called me Gator before," he said.

"But isn't that what your sister always called you?"

"Yes." He paused. "But you're not my sister. My name is Ken."

I hugged him and spoke in his ear. "And my name is really Clyde. But don't tell anyone else. They wouldn't believe that a robot's positronic brain could be repaired."

He drew back in wonder. "Are you—?"

"Shh." I put a finger to his lips. "It's a secret just between you and me."

A light shone in his face. Then he snapped forward to bite my finger. But I was too quick for him and he missed. He laughed.

"You knew I was going to do that," he said, delighted.

"Yeah, I know about you and your alligator teeth." I smiled and messed up his hair. "I remember that much."

Look for Christopher Pike's
The Visitor
Coming mid-October 1995

About the Author

CHRISTOPHER PIKE was born in Brooklyn, New York, but grew up in Los Angeles, where he lives to this day. Prior to becoming a writer, he worked in a factory, painted houses, and programmed computers. His hobbies include astronomy, meditating, running, playing with his nieces and nephews, and making sure his books are prominently displayed in local bookstores. He is the author of *Last Act, Spellbound, Gimme a Kiss, Remember Me, Scavenger Hunt, Final Friends* 1, 2, and 3, *Fall into Darkness, See You Later, Witch, Die Softly, Bury Me Deep, Whisper of Death, Chain Letter 2: The Ancient Evil, Master of Murder, Monster, Road to Nowhere, The Eternal Enemy, The Immortal, The Wicked Heart, The Midnight Club, The Last Vampire, The Last Vampire 2: Black Blood, The Last Vampire 3: Red Dice, Remember Me 2: The Return, Remember Me 3: The Last Story,* and *The Lost Mind,* all available from Archway Paperbacks. *Slumber Party, Weekend, Chain Letter,* and *Sati*—an adult novel about a very unusual lady—are also by Mr. Pike.